WONDERLAND

MIRANDA RENAE

Immortal Works LLC
1505 Glenrose Drive
Salt Lake City, Utah 84104
Tel: (385) 202-0116

Cover Art by Ashley Literski
http://strangedevotion.wixsite.com/strangedesigns

ISBN B08DC6WRC8 (Paperback)
ASIN 978-1-7349046-7-3 (Kindle Edition)

Chapter 1

He wore black leather gloves to hide his fingerprints, but he could still feel the cold padlock in his hands. "This is the job," he said to himself. The phrase had been his mantra since the moment his father took the contract with Red Queen Inc. and recruited him to do the "computer stuff." Not that that was what he was doing now.

"Rabbit." His father's voice crackled through the walkie on his hip. "Stop daydreaming."

On the red-orange wall behind him, tiny white lights surrounded a poster of the newest movie. All but one glowed bright. He stared at the burnt-out bulb and the red light of the tiny camera blinking at him. If it had been one of his brothers sitting behind the monitor, he would have raised his middle finger in a sarcastic, "Love you, too." But the old man would never stand for that.

Rabbit removed the walkie from his hip. "On my way."

The squeak of his sneakers echoed through the empty lobby. He stopped before exiting the theater, looking at the doors he'd padlocked shut. *Do the people inside know they're lab rats? Not that it matters. It's happening.* He pushed through the glass doors and stepped into the chill winter wind; a cold tingle spread across his uncovered cheeks.

Rabbit stared at the broken sign of the pawnshop across the

street. Its windows were covered in cardboard that trapped the light from inside, he sighed inward. It was going to be a long couple of hours in their temporary operations headquarters. *Only 208 days and I'll be eighteen. Then I'm free.*

He crossed the street and walked around the building, looking around before tapping three times on the silver rolling door that had once been used as a loading bay. It was now the only entrance into the building. Faded red letters of the former owner's name were painted across the metal slats. Rabbit waited for the door to make its slow ascent, thinking of the life he could have had. A normal life. Working part-time as a cashier, going to school, hanging out with friends. If his mother hadn't... He shook the memory from his mind. *No, I'm not going there. Not now. Not ever.*

The *clink, clink, clink* of the door stopped, and he stepped into the dark, murky warehouse, leaving the smells of the crisp winter air and fresh popcorn behind him. Without making eye contact, he walked past his father toward the main part of the gutted-out pawnshop. A freckled girl sat in front of a wall of brightly lit computer screens. Her laptop was next to his on the long red-and-white folding table set up below the wall screens. Rabbit let himself smile, not only because his father wasn't as aggressive if he had an audience—and the boss's sister was definitely an audience—but also because Rabbit liked spending time with her. He walked across the stained floor and plopped down in the chair next to her. "Hey."

Dinah looked up with a wide smile. "Hey, Rabbit."

"Ahem." The dark shadow that could only be his father moved between them. His father looked down at him. "Camera three." Rabbit looked up at the screen but didn't see anything wrong with it. Before he could say anything, his father's phone rang, and he moved back into the shadows to answer it. Rabbit rolled his eyes.

Dinah, used to his father's bad manners, spoke as if nothing had happened. "I saved you Red Vines." Her high ponytail bounced as she spoke. "But it'll cost you."

Rabbit knew what she wanted: Dinah was a bubble gum addict,

and her sister wouldn't let her have it. It had been almost six months since he'd last worked with her, but he still kept gum on him. Just in case. Dinah slid the open package of candy across the table to him. He tapped a few keys on his laptop before sliding the bright pink gum package to her.

Rabbit and Dinah both jumped when a big yellow purse fell onto the table between them. The silvery voice of Reid Redding, the CEO of Red Queen Inc., rang through the room. "Are the cameras up and running?"

His father stammered, "Yes, ma'am." Ms. Redding made Rabbit's father nervous. That was something Rabbit and his father had in common.

She stood between Rabbit and Dinah. "Show me." Before answering, Rabbit put a piece of the sweet, chewy candy in his mouth to calm his nerves. It had the added bonus of pissing his father off. *It's not professional to eat on the job.*

"There are five cameras in the lobby, ten in the theater, and one at each exit point." Rabbit pointed at the wall of screens in front of them.

Ms. Redding examined the screens. "This needs to be perfect." She pointed to a black screen. "What about this one?"

Dinah put a new piece of gum in her mouth. "That's the projection room." Only a sliver of light shone from under the door. "It's usually empty once the movie starts." She popped her gum, and Ms. Redding glared at her, but Dinah went on as if nothing had happened. "We put a camera in there just in case." Dinah smiled at her sister before looking back at the screen, letting her fingers move across the keyboard, the clicking keys filling the silence of the room.

Ms. Redding leaned in close to the largest screen, which was filled with a panoramic view of the entire theater. "Joe, I don't want a repeat of last time."

"Of course not, ma'am," Rabbit's father replied. "We've taken every precaution to prevent that."

Like having your son break the law and padlock a room full of people? Rabbit still wasn't sure why. It wasn't like anything terrible happened last time or even the time before that, but when Joseph told you to do something, you did it.

Satisfied with Joseph's answer, Ms. Redding moved away from the screen and turned to her sister. "Have you seen Elizabeth?"

Having met Dr. Elizabeth Smith only once, Rabbit wasn't sure if he could find her in the crowded theater, but he'd try if only to keep the sisters from arguing. He scanned the screens in front of him, looking for the raven-haired doctor.

"I haven't seen her yet," Dinah said. "Maybe she's not coming."

There was movement on the screen in the far right corner of the abandoned parking lot of the pawnshop. The new blue car looked out of place among the broken pavement and discarded shopping carts. Rabbit enlarged the picture on the big screen in the center of the room. Dr. Smith and a teenage girl stood next to the car. The girl had long dark hair, and Rabbit assumed she was Dr. Smith's daughter, Alice. Alice was wearing a sundress despite the fact that it was the middle of winter and the ground was covered in two inches of snow. Her dark blue leggings with bright silver stars would do nothing against the cold. She shivered, pulling the thin jean jacket closer around her as she yelled at her mother.

Rabbit pointed at the screen. "Looks like they're in the parking lot."

Ms. Redding grabbed her purse and started toward the door. "Dinah," she called out in a tone that demanded her sister follow.

Dinah stood up to follow her sister, but before she left, she leaned down and whispered in Rabbit's ear. "You always did have a knack for finding a beautiful girl." Heat moved across his neck to his cheek; he hated that Dinah could make him blush.

Ms. Redding rushed out to meet the guest of honor. Her clacking heels echoed through the nearly empty warehouse. Dinah and his father followed close behind.

Alone, Rabbit pulled up the audio for the camera in the parking lot.

"Alice Marie Smith, you wanted to go to this movie. Now you... what?" Dr. Smith asked her daughter. "Don't feel like it?"

The dark-haired girl played with something on her wrist. "I..." She shrugged. "I don't know. Okay?"

Dr. Smith's face fell, and her shoulders slumped. She moved toward the girl. Alice backed away from her mother, her jaw clenched and face red. She was mumbling something under her breath.

"Breathe, Alice." Dr. Smith took a step toward her. "You're fine."

The girl didn't move this time. She glared at her mother and started counting. "One, two, three..." Her chest rose with each number. Each breath seemed to calm her, changing her. Her rigid posture relaxed with the rise of her chest, and the redness drained from her face.

Dr. Smith moved closer, pulling her daughter into a hug. "We don't have—"

Ms. Redding's silvery voice came through the microphone. "There you are."

He'd forgotten about Ms. Redding, gotten too involved in what was happening between Dr. Smith and her daughter.

Dinah came into view. She glared at her sister, frustration flashing across her face at Ms. Redding's lack of tact. Ms. Redding didn't acknowledge her, and Dinah rolled her eyes and turned to face Dr. Smith. "We were worried you weren't going to make it."

Alice flashed Dinah a movie-star smile, with bright white teeth and red lips that held a bit of mystery. Rabbit couldn't help but smile himself. "Sorry, it was my fault." She motioned to her outfit. "I couldn't find anything to wear."

Dinah laughed. "I completely understand. Love the tights, by the way." She held her hand out to Alice. "Name's Dinah, but I prefer DeeDee." She glanced at her sister. "Only family and people who have known me forever call me Dinah."

Dr. Smith smiled at Alice and Dinah. "Should we go in, then?" she asked.

The four women moved toward the back of the theater, to the only door that had not been blocked off. *Yet.* Rabbit switched the screen back to show a view of all the cameras on one screen. He scanned each one for anyone who didn't belong in the area, though he wasn't too worried; the location had been chosen with the knowledge that it was near-abandoned, and Joseph had made sure that only those with tickets to the event could get in. The movie theater and a bar a few blocks down were the only buildings still open, and Rabbit would bet the people in the bar were also employed by the Redding family.

Rabbit watched the screens for twenty minutes, looking for any changes. A flash of movement on one of the screens caught his attention. Dinah and Ms. Redding stepped out of a gray door and pushed it closed, and his father moved in behind them, screwing a thick board across the door, sealing the only exit from the theater.

The clink of the metal door in the back of the building rang through the room, followed by the clacking of Ms. Redding's heels. Rabbit changed the main screen from the street out front to the large theater.

He knew the drill. Ms. Redding would want to see and hear everything that was happening in that theater. In preparation, he turned up the sound on the main screen. Moments later, a yellow bag fell onto the table next to him, and Ms. Redding collapsed into a nearby chair as the movie started.

It was one of those movies based on one of his favorite comic books, one Rabbit would have loved to watch. Maybe with Dinah. Or Alice. He looked for the girl with the bright smile. Alice sat in the front row between her mother and a skinny guy with thick-framed glasses. A large popcorn bucket sat on her lap with a headdress of Red Vines sticking out of the top, and her eyes were focused on the screen. Alice's laugh tinkled through the audience, and Rabbit's lips moved into a smile.

Dinah plopped down in the chair next to him, smelling of popcorn and fresh air. "Anything happened yet?" she asked.

He looked away from Alice and scanned the theater. "Not yet."

As if on cue, a thin layer of pinkish-red smoke rolled along the carpeted theater stairs. It cascaded down each step, clinging to its unsuspecting victims. Pooling on the cold, sticky floor, the smoke built in both thickness and height the longer it sat.

Rabbit had watched this experiment five times, and he still wasn't sure what was supposed to happen.

The smoke rose, settling on the laps of the people in the front rows, and he waited for someone to call out, but like every other experiment, no one said anything.

The guy with the glasses sitting next to Alice stood up. Rabbit slumped back in his chair. This was it. The end of the experiment. He would yell "Fire!" and mass hysteria would ensue, like last time, only this time the doors were blocked. He didn't want to think about what would happen to the people in the theater when they realized this.

Rabbit watched the glasses guy move closer to Alice. Standing over her, staring down at her, he cracked his knuckles. Rabbit sat up and moved closer to the screen to see what she would do. Alice looked around the room, confusion clear on her face.

Glasses Guy moved closer to Alice, his face inches from hers. "Because I'm not," he spat.

Alice scrunched down into the maroon theater chair. Rabbit gripped the handles of his chair tightly to keep himself from running in and rescuing her. *Her mother is with her,* he reminded himself. *She'll protect Alice. Besides, you can't get in. All the doors are blocked.*

Dr. Smith stood up, and Rabbit loosened his grip as she turned toward the guy. That's when Rabbit saw it, the change in her face: the light of intelligence, of forward-thinking, blinked out.

A guttural roar filled the speakers. Dr. Smith moved to the front of the theater, her face filling one of the screens as she got near a camera.

The roar had come from Dr. Smith.

Rabbit changed the camera angle to get a better view of the room, bringing up the movie screen for a split second. The red cape of the comic hero jutted across the screen almost as if mocking him. *I'm not a hero; I'm a villain*, Rabbit thought. He focused the camera on the larger room. *Or at the very least a minion.*

The pinkish smoke covered the top half of the theater. A scruff of hair from one of the taller people was the only thing visible in the wall of cotton candy–like smoke. A woman's voice—the superhero's love interest—echoed through the room moments before Dr. Smith's polished voice drowned out the sounds of the movie as she screamed, "My stars and whiskers."

The smoke cleared, and Dinah tapped on the keyboard next to Rabbit, zooming in on Dr. Smith's face. A river of red-black blood streamed from her emotionless blue eyes. Her lips moved in what Rabbit hoped was a silent prayer, but he knew from the flush of her skin and the clenching of her fist that they weren't.

The camera zoomed out, still staying focused on Dr. Smith. The pink smoke had transformed into a pink powder that now littered the floor. Rabbit tried to find Alice. *I want to... I don't know.* His heart pounded in his ears. *Why am I so worried about this girl? She's a stranger.* But at the same time, she wasn't. It was in Dr. Smith's file. Two brothers she barely saw and a parent who... Well, it didn't matter. Alice was like him.

The movie screen flashed with an explosion that lit the room, drawing Rabbit's view to the far corner. A girl with star tights was curled up under the big screen. Her arms wrapped around her knees as she rocked back and forth. Rabbit concentrated on Alice, willing her to find a better place to hide. A loud scream echoed through the room, and Alice clasped her hands over her ears, her mouth moving, making the shapes of words. One, two, three. *Alice is counting.*

Dr. Smith turned toward her daughter. A war cry left her bloodstained throat, and it sent cold dread down Rabbit's spine. He watched, unable to look away from the screen, as Dr. Smith stumbled, zombie-like, toward Alice. He was transfixed by the impending disaster, frozen by fear.

Dr. Smith raised her fisted hands in an arch above her daughter.

The screen went black.

What happened?

Ms. Redding pounded on the desk next to him. "Get it back."

Rabbit tore his gaze from the black screens, his fingers racing across the keyboard. An image of Alice's face burned into his mind. He scrolled through line after line of code as Ms. Redding's heels clacked on the floor behind him. Next to him, Dinah didn't move. She stared at the black screen, her breath heavy and labored. Rabbit stopped typing, turning to check on Dinah.

Joseph grasped his shoulders, and in a harsh tone that Rabbit knew was best to listen to, he demanded that Rabbit get back to work.

It took some time, but he found it, a small coding error, something that hadn't been there before. He'd checked the feed himself earlier that morning. His hand shook as he typed in a fix. It took three times of pressing keys in the wrong order before he got it right.

The screen came to life with a flash.

In the time they had lost the picture, the entire theater had transformed into a mass of bloody, screaming humanoid forms. It was like the start of a bad zombie movie, only this was real life. Ignoring the broken chairs and scattered popcorn that littered the sticky floor, Rabbit tried to look past the lifeless eyes for the girl in the white dress.

The movie screen came into view, a close-up on the villain's face, monologuing. But no Alice. He switched the cameras, the drumming of his heart drowning out the sounds of the theater and Ms. Redding's screaming orders.

He needed to find her. *She had to be okay.*

The camera panned to the center of the room. Dr. Smith stood in the aisle, her T-shirt and jeans covered in red blobs of... *I don't want to know.* Long dark hair curled around her long fingers. Dark red blood dripped down her arms. The jean jacket that Alice had been wearing lay at her feet.

The screen went dark.

Again.

This time, Rabbit did nothing to fix it. He was afraid of what he would find. Ms. Redding raged behind him. Venomous words about his incompetence rolled off her tongue. He ignored them. It wasn't the first time he'd heard them.

Dinah sniffled next to him. Rabbit turned to her. Thick black lines of makeup marked her tear-soaked cheeks. She was crying—not a silent cry, but a full, desperate hyperventilating cry. Rabbit rubbed his eyes and realized his face was wet with tears as well.

Ms. Redding's short brown hair came into view. She pushed her way between Rabbit and Dinah and started pressing buttons on Dinah's keyboard. "Where is it?" she yelled inches from Dinah's face.

Rabbit stood up and put himself between the siblings. He knew what had happened to the feed, even suspected it when it happened the first time, but looking at Dinah, now he was sure. Dinah had killed the feed, and he was thankful for it. No one should die like that. The fact that Ms. Redding wanted to watch the carnage terrified him.

What had Joseph gotten them into?

Ms. Redding pushed her sister out of the way and pounding on the keys. When the screen didn't change, she yelled at Rabbit, "Get it back."

He looked at Ms. Redding and his father, who had moved to stand next to her. Rabbit met his father's stoic gaze. "I can't," he lied.

His dad nodded.

Relieved, Rabbit took that as an agreement and moved to kneel in front of Dinah. *I can't watch anymore.* Rabbit pushed the hair that had come loose from Dinah's ponytail from her face. She was still struggling to breathe, and her eyes had a faraway look.

"Dinah," he said. "Breathe." She took a deep breath, and another, a far-off look in her eyes. Rabbit pulled her into his arms and let her cry.

He wasn't sure how long they sat like that, Ms. Redding barking orders to get feedback up, him ignoring her, while his dad stood between the crazed CEO and her sister.

When Dinah calmed down enough to reason, she made a call to Red Queen's cleanup crew and their lawyer. Fewer than ten minutes passed before the cleanup team arrived at the movie theater, almost as if they had been waiting for a call, maybe in the bar down the street.

Dinah turned on the cameras, restoring the feed she'd cut earlier. A black van with a red heart on the side pulled up to the building and parked on the sidewalk in front of the glass doors. Men in white hazmat suits stepped out of the sliding door of the van and pushed their way through the theater doors.

A weighted silence held the room as they watch the cleanup crew progress through the theater. When they stopped at the double doors —the doors Rabbit had threaded with heavy chains hours before—he turned his back to the screen, unable to acknowledge his part. The loud clang of the metal chain hitting the tile outside the door echoed through the camera's microphone. The Red Vines that Rabbit had eaten earlier rolled over in his stomach, threatening to make a reappearance. *What would have happened if I hadn't blocked that door?*

Keeping his eyes down, Rabbit grabbed his laptop and shoved it into his backpack. He didn't want to see the cleanup. The images of the dead, broken, and blood-soaked bodies that littered the room would haunt his nightmares for the rest of his life. *Will I be able to leave? Or get locked away somewhere? Will Ms. Redding have me killed?* He shoved the open package of Red Vines into his bag. It didn't matter. He couldn't live in the same house as the man who had helped kill dozens of people.

Rabbit pushed his hands through his thick blond curls. *I'm as guilty as he is in those people's deaths.*

A muffled voice crackled across his father's walkie. "We have a survivor."

Rabbit looked up at the screen.

A girl stood in the front of the room, silhouetted by the bright lights above and the white letters of the credits behind her. She held her bare arms in front of her, the palms of her hands turned up. The once white dress was stained the same red of the floor and walls around her. With a few keystrokes, Dinah zoomed in on the girl's face. Her eyes held a wealth of emotion—most of all, fear.

Her name left Rabbit's lips without his permission. "Alice."

Chapter 2

Four years later

Alice pulled the comforter over her head, hiding from the orange rays of the early morning sun peeking through the heavy woven curtains. Today was the day of the big trip to Red Rocks, and she knew she should get up, even if her alarm had yet to go off. The night before had been a late one—meetings, classes, and overseeing the packing had kept her out well past two.

Barenaked Ladies blared through her phone, bouncing off the white brick walls of her dorm room. Alice grabbed her phone from the desk that was next to her bed with the tips of her fingers, the only things to leave her cocoon. *The lack of makeup would be worth fifteen minutes more.* Without opening an eye, she swiped left, snoozing the alarm. Then she slid the phone under her pillow.

Her mind floated back to the dream she'd been having before the Ladies had so rudely awoken her. Kaleb stood in front of her, his big blue eyes sparkling with love, a deep red rose on a white lace table between them. He clasped her hand in his. "Alice?"

Alice was pulled from her dream by the *Vworp! Vworp!* of the Tardis signaling an incoming message from Kaleb. The sound reminded her of the first time Kaleb had watched *Doctor Who*; he was sure it was the weirdest thing he had ever seen. Now he spent every Saturday night on her couch watching it.

With the blanket still over her head, Alice pulled the phone from under her pillow. Her fingers moved across the dots, making a backward check mark that would unlock the screen. Alice had a feeling Kaleb's text would be something like "I'm running late." He was always late. The small screen lit up her blanket-covered cave, giving it an unearthly blue glow.

Ace, running late, can you catch a ride with Linc?
Ps, I hope you planned for extra people.

She let out a frustrated breath to stop her vision from flickering to black and white. It wasn't that she was upset because he was late—she'd planned for that. Alice started to count, her way of dealing with her irrational feelings of anger and the flickering that accompanied them since that day in the theater.

One, two, three.

The problem was that she had to plan for extra people. *It's not that big of a deal*, she reminded herself. *This happens all the time. You've even planned for it.* With a forced smile, Alice punched in her response to Kaleb.

Sure and I did.

No longer able to sleep, Alice pushed the blankets from her face, placed the phone back on the desk she used as a nightstand, and stared up at the ceiling. It was covered in posters and drawings that wouldn't stick to the glossy white painted brick walls of her room. They were mostly movie posters of cult classics, like *Killer Klowns from Outer Space*, *SLC Punk!*, *Speed Racer*, and in the center of her collage, her coveted *Goonies* poster.

Vworp! Vworp!

Great. I'll let Linc know. You're the best.

She sat up and pushed her shoulder-length brown hair from her eyes. *The best. That's me.* It shouldn't have annoyed her, but the statement did. She knew Kaleb didn't mean for it to be patronizing, but it was.

The ride with Linc and Tom wouldn't be horrible.

Alice slid down the side of her cinder-block-raised bed, placing her cell phone in the pocket of her pajama bottoms.

She'd been looking forward to spending time with Kaleb, without roommates or his brothers, neither of which were allowed in his "baby," a black '83 Camaro with T-top that he affectionately called Dorothy. Now she would have to spend the two hours it took to get to the campsite in the uncovered Jeep. *On the freeway. Ugh.* She hated the ringing in her ears that accompanied a long drive without the protection of doors and windows.

Alice opened the door to her bedroom. The smell of coffee overwhelmed her, reminding Alice of her childhood, of Sunday mornings playing with her brothers while her parents sat on the porch talking about their week. Things had changed so much since then, and that was before her mom had died. But now was not the time to think about that. Alice followed the soft hum of music that came from behind the closed door of the kitchen, noticing the bedroom door across the hall from her room stood open, both beds empty.

She padded down the hall, the worn carpet rough under her bare feet, walking past the bathroom she shared with her three other roommates. The kitchen door opened with a squeak, bringing with it the sound of smooth jazz. *I hope Marci wasn't up all night studying again,* she thought.

It was Kit, Marci's twin sister, who sat at the kitchen table, not Marci. Textbooks and notepads lay open on every available space. Handwritten note cards, highlighted in bright blues and pinks, littered the bench that served as seating for the kitchen table, and a textbook sat on top of a large pot.

Kit looked up from her computer screen. "Fresh pot." She nodded toward the coffee maker on the counter.

"Thanks," Alice muttered.

She pulled the kitchen door closed behind her, not wanting to wake their other roommate. *Not that the noise would wake her.* The girl had slept through the fire alarm going off for twenty minutes after one of the boys in D Hall set something on fire.

Alice opened the cupboard above the coffee pot to grab a mug. An orange sticky note with the first two lines of Romeo and Juliet written on it floated down to the counter. She stuck the note back on the cupboard door before grabbing a black mug.

The coffee flowed from the pot to the cup, filling the air with its rich aroma. Alice leaned back on the counter, taking her first sip of the dark brew. With that one sip, the stress and anxiety of the coming events washed away. She moved across the room to sit on a clear spot on the bench across from Kit. A picture of President Roosevelt stared up at her from a US history book on the table. Under the picture was a pink Post-it with a complicated math problem scrawled across it.

"Have you seen..." Kit grabbed the pink Post-it. "There it is."

This wasn't the first time Alice had seen Kit study; bright-colored notes littered the common rooms they shared. Today was the first time Alice had looked at what she was studying. A chemistry book sat open on top of the microwave. More Post-it notes with what looked like Shakespeare printed on them covered the back of the kitchen door, and an assortment of multicolored pens were spread around the room. "How do you study like this?" Alice asked.

Kit looked up from her laptop, eyes glazed over in a study haze. She blinked a few times before Alice saw her question register. "Everything is color coded. Pink for chemistry, yellow for history, and so on."

Alice looked around the room. "Okay, but how do you keep track of everything? There are notes and books everywhere. I even found a stack of blue and green index cards in the fridge last night."

Kit stood up and moved around the table to the fridge. "Organized chaos."

"If you say so." Alice laughed. "But index cards in the fridge?"

"Don't laugh." Kit opened the fridge and pulled out the cards. "Someday these cards could save your life." She put the cards on the counter and poured herself a new cup of coffee. "Hey, isn't your big camping trip today?"

Alice stood up and placed her empty cup in the sink. "Yep. Still not coming?"

"I have to study. I'm behind." Kit looked around the room with a frown. "After the disaster of Hurricane Adam, I can't, not if I want to graduate on time."

Alice nodded, remembering the mess Kit had been when Marci and Kaleb brought her to live here. Adam had been a real jerk, the type that you wished would fall in a hole somewhere and never come out.

The buzz of Alice's phone made them both jump. *I need to get a different text tone for Tom.* She pulled the phone from her pocket.

Hey Cupcake, Linc wants to know if you will meet our friend Ryan at B Hall. We'll pick you up there in an hour or so.

"Is that Kaleb?" Kit asked.

Alice shook her head. "No, Tom. He wants me to meet their friend Ryan at B Hall."

"Isn't that the hall that ran off the RA?" Kit asked.

"I think so."

The phone chirped again.

Ryan's the new RA. He'll be wearing a white cowboy hat.

Of course, he'll be wearing a white cowboy hat, Alice thought. *I wonder if he'll have an accent, and if he does, will he try to hide it like Linc?* She looked up from her phone; Kit had moved to sit behind her computer again, her long dark hair covering her face. Alice said, "Guess Ryan's the new B Hall RA."

"That sucks."

Alice smiled.

The alarm on her phone sang out a heart-pounding techno song. She didn't know the song or words, but it was one of Kaleb's favorites, which was why Alice picked it. It was her if-you-don't-get-up-now-then-there-is-no-reason-to-get-up-at-all-because-you're-beyond-late alarm. Alice shut it off and started back to her room.

Kit stopped her at the door, asking, "What weird food thing did Tom call you this time?"

"Cupcake."

"That wasn't very original. He must be off his game. "

Alice shrugged. "He'll have something weirder later, I'm sure."

ALICE WOULDN'T HAVE ENTERED this building if she hadn't agreed to meet Linc's friend here. The smell coming through the open entryway doors was enough to scare off any sane person. Plugging her nose, she walked through the doors and up to the second floor. Red sand and remnants of multicolored water balloons littered the stairwell. The dried dirt mixed with mud crunched and swished under the white soles of her purple Converse, making a *whoosh-chomp* noise that reminded Alice of a mud monster in a B-grade horror movie. Alice stopped next to the big white door that stood open, revealing the long hallway of B Hall. Six doors along each wall stood open, the contents of each room spilling into the hallway. Books, chairs, and paper plates created a haphazard path through a sea of empty energy drink cans. It reminded Alice of the times she had played the lava game with her younger brothers.

She looked down at her watch, wondering where Linc's friend was. "I bet they ate him, savages," she mumbled.

Behind her, a low gravelly voice said, "I was thinking a pagan sacrifice."

She turned to face the man behind the voice, a hand on her chest and a tentative smile on her lips.

"I'm sorry, sugar, didn't mean to scare you," he said.

She examined the stranger. Dark curly hair cut short, hazel eyes, and freckles that speckled the bridge of his nose to his cheeks. She had always had a thing for freckles. He wore blue jeans, sneakers, and a bright pink shirt with the words "Real men wear pink" in thick black letters scrolled across the chest. He held a white cowboy hat between his tan, weather-worn hands.

"Ryan?" she asked.

"Yes, ma'am." He took one of her hands in his and smiled at her, his white teeth shining like a beacon. "Alice, it's nice to meet you." He moved their joined hands to his lips, kissing the top of her hand.

Ryan's soft pink lips rested on the top of her hand, causing a warm pink blush to spread across Alice's fair skin. She'd seen this in movies a thousand times. The girl was supposed to swoon or something like that. It should have been even a little romantic, but in truth, it was awkward.

The act changed from awkward to disgusting when his mouth opened into an O shape and he began to suck, his white teeth scraping the top layers of her skin.

The *thump-thump* of her heart sounded in her ears. She took a deep breath, trying to calm herself, and scanned the room, looking for an exit. She tried to tug her hand away, but his grip tightened, and Alice's vision flickered from Technicolor to black and white. The anger hidden beneath the surface of her normally calm exterior bubbled up, overriding the fear of what would happen if she let it take control.

The color drained from the room as if a black-and-white TV show had come to life. Alice scanned the room, looking for something. *For what?* She wasn't sure. A scrap of color caught her eye. Beckoned her.

The scarlet fire extinguisher glowed red in her black-and-white world.

Alice stared at it and imagined the cold steel against her heated skin. A grin moved across her lips, and a delicious shiver ran through her body. She thought of the things she could do with that red steel. Her feet turned toward the bewitching cylinder. Alice saw herself skipping toward it, a twisted and cold smile on her lips, imagining the weight of it in her soft hands and the confused look on Ryan's angelic face moments before she—no, she wasn't going to go there.

She took a deep, labored breath to try to keep the image of what came next from appearing, but reality had faded into a world of calculated fury. The slideshow of her plan took hold, keeping Alice's rational mind hostage.

She raised the improvised weapon above her head, a rattlesnake ready to strike its victim. A single thought crossed her muddled mind. *It's heavier than it looks.* That thought sent beads of pleasure through her fevered body. The fire extinguisher moved in a slow arch, meeting its target, spurts of dark crimson blood and broken white teeth falling to the litter-covered floor. A sense of freedom came over her. *No more holding back.*

Alice took a step back, away from Ryan, toward the fire extinguisher, ready to play out the twisted images running through her mind. The excitement of not having to clamp down her anger, the hunger of it, was like a drug.

"Darling?" Ryan's smooth voice broke through Alice's nightmare.

She blinked, his undamaged freckled face coming into view. Alice took a deep breath, the air helping her think. *Do I actually want to do this?*

Alice concentrated on the air moving through her lungs, expanding, contracting. Colors came back with each labored breath, bringing with them reality—a reality where Ryan still held her hand, his wet lips hanging above it and a toothy grin on his face.

Alice yanked it away. She mumbled her mantra. "It's fine." *Had he just...yuck.* Alice wiped her sticky, slobbery hand on her favorite jeans before meeting his dark eyes. "What is wrong with you?"

A wide smile spread across his face. He shrugged as if he had done nothing wrong, his wide, toothy cat-like grin mocking her.

Alice threw her hands in the air before stomping down the stairs and through the heavy glass door. She counted as she went, trying to keep her control. *One, two, three, four...* Ryan called for her to wait up. She picked up her pace; gray sidewalk blurred around her, and catcalls from the boys playing volleyball formed a static in the background of her escape.

Thirty-four, thirty-five, thirty-six...

Tom's ugly black Jeep was in her sight, Linc's dark hair visible in the front passenger seat. Anger rose inside her at the sight of Linc. *He asked me to wait for his creepy friend.* Alice looked over at the driver's seat. At Tom. *No, it wasn't Linc who asked me to meet his friend; it was Tom.* Anger washed over Alice as she watched his dark hair bounce in time to the blaring music coming from the Jeep. Normally she liked Kaleb's roommates, but today the Sanchez brothers were as guilty of Ryan's crimes as Ryan.

The smile, the one that makes every girl Linc meets melt, will not work. Not this time. Not on me.

The rap music blaring from the Jeep shook the ground around the car. Alice yanked open the passenger-side door ready to... She didn't know, but it wasn't going to be nice. Linc clasped onto the metal frame of the door, trying not to fall out on top of her, his bright teal shirt nearly blinding Alice.

"What the heck, Alice?" Linc yelled over the music.

Alice looked from Tom, with his stupid grin, to Linc, who stared down at her with a look of confusion. The toad Ryan had caught up to her, laughter still shining in his eyes, and Alice knew she'd been played. Her vision flickered from color to black and white, and she took a deep breath. *I'm fine. I won't let them know they got to me.*

"Sorry, Linc, I didn't realize you were sitting so close to the door." She looked up at him, trying to convince him with her eyes that their little pranks hadn't affected her while she planned what she was going to do to get back at them. "Do you mind if I sit in front?" She put her hands on her stomach. "I get carsick."

"Sure."

Linc exchanged a look with his brother and got out of the Jeep. He pushed Ryan into the back seat behind Tom and then climbed into the seat behind what was now Alice's seat. Out of habit she adjusted the seat to give Linc legroom before Tom put the Jeep in reverse.

Linc's dark hair appeared between the seats, and he tried to hand her his phone. "Shotgun chooses the music," he said.

Alice shook her head. "Thanks, but I brought my own." There was no way Alice could handle two hours of the same boring rhythmic noise Linc and Tom called music. She thumbed through her playlist, trying to find the music that fit her mood. The red wings of a butterfly on a pearl backdrop popped up on her screen. Linc groaned behind her, and Alice knew what the perfect revenge would be. Alice pressed play, filling the car with the alluring sounds of *Madam Butterfly*.

"Opera," Tom whined.

Alice beamed. "It's my favorite."

Two hours later they pulled into the campsite.

The drive hadn't been as bad as she thought it would be. The opera caused a degree of torment that gratified her need for revenge. Her skin crawled at the thought of Ryan's lips on her hand. Yuck.

Tom parked the Jeep behind the big white truck Alice had helped pack the night before. She didn't know how long the others had been there, but the truck was still stuffed with gear and groceries, and no one was around. Not that she was surprised. Alice pulled on the door handle, ready to get out of the Jeep and unload everything herself, but before she could jump out, Ryan's big head moved between her and Tom's seat.

"Alice?"

She couldn't help but glare at him. "What?"

Ryan handed her a crisp green bill, Benjamin Franklin's big eyes and wavy hair staring at her. What was he trying to do? Buy her friendship? Silence? What was this guy's game? Whatever it was, a hundred bucks was not going to do it. She looked at him, waiting for an explanation.

He shifted in his seat. "Tom and Linc told me about your manners...or...what they like to call your legendary calm. You know how..." He fidgeted. "A... Well, they said no matter how gross or rude someone is, you will smile politely." He rubbed the back of his neck. "Make conversation and never mention their actions." He looked over at Tom. "So... Well... Um... We had this bet, Tom and me."

Alice raised her eyebrow but didn't say anything. Linc's dark eyes met hers in the rearview mirror.

"I had nothing to do with it," he blurted.

Alice knew better. "Besides knowing about it and, I'm guessing here, holding the money," she said.

Linc looked down before saying, "Something like that."

Alice glared at all three of them, each of them unable to meet her eyes. "So... A hundred bucks and all you had to do was lick me?"

Tom blurted out, "Dude, you licked her?"

Ryan smiled that same wide, charm-filled smile he had used before the incident. "Best money I've ever made." He looked toward Alice, not meeting her eyes. "That Alice made."

"Argh." Alice threw open the door and dropped the bill on the seat. Though tempted to keep the money, she knew it would encourage them. She heard about their "epic" pranks from Kaleb, usually stupid drunken bets resulting in ER visits for second-degree burns and stitches. One of them had even been branded with a hot dog skewer. Alice had never been the recipient of their pranks, and she'd never wanted to be. "I'm going down to the lake; you three can unload the truck."

Alice made her way through the camp to a nearby trail, going over what had happened in her head. *Why would they bet on whether I would react or not? Of course, I would,* she thought. *Someone licks you, and you react.* She sat down on a log and stared out onto the calm waters of the lake. *It's not like I never show emotions. So I don't lose my temper or even cry in front of them.* She preferred to do that in the privacy of her room or her car. *That doesn't mean I'm a robot who never feels anything. Besides, nothing good comes from feeling too much, at least not for me. It was bad before that day at the theater, but now that the WonderLand virus runs through my veins, it's even more dangerous. I could lose control at any moment. I almost did it with Ryan.*

A cold sweat settled on Alice's skin as she tried to push back the memories of that horrible day, the day she lost her mother and watched everyone around her kill each other.

She took a deep breath, the scent of earth, trees, and water surrounding her. Alice unlaced her shoes, rolled up the legs of her jeans, and removed her socks, letting sand squish between her toes with every step she took toward the deep blue water. She concentrated on the beauty that surrounded her and let the sun's rays ease into her, washing away the thoughts of cold winter days and the memories that haunted her.

Alice stood at the water's edge for what seemed like minutes but was more like an hour. The water lapping at the red gravel shore brought peace to the chaos of her virus-crazed emotions. The waves took with them the fear of her almost loss of control and the visions of what she could do. Sunrays twinkled on the water's surface as she sighed and watched the dragonflies dance in the light's silent song. She took a final calming breath before starting back to camp.

As she approached the camp, a familiar engine roared nearby, and butterflies turned in her stomach. *Kaleb.* Alice rushed to meet the one person she had wanted to see today. Kaleb's blond mop of curls peeked out of an open window. A warm smile spread across his face when he saw Alice. She loved his smile.

"Hey, Ace, sorry we're late," Kaleb called out to Alice.

Alice opened her mouth, ready to make a joke about how he was always late when the word *we* registered.

In the passenger seat sat a tall blonde girl Alice had not invited. On purpose. The calm she'd found at the lake evaporated at the sight of DeeDee. Every time Alice saw her, all she could think about was how DeeDee and her sister had left her to die. *That's not fair. They couldn't have known what would happen, and DeeDee has been nothing but nice to me,* Alice reminded herself. *She's always willing to help, even if it interrupts her life. Besides, she's one of Kaleb's oldest friends.*

It's not her fault you can't get past that she had been in the theater, leaving moments before the chaos started.

DeeDee stepped out of the car, her long legs covered in a skirt, and Kaleb moved around the car to stand next to her. "Where is everyone?"

She looked around the campsite. It should be packed. There had been at least twenty people who had said they were coming. But all she saw was Linc, Tom, and Ryan sitting around a bonfire. Not even Jack, the owner of the white truck she had helped pack, had returned to camp.

"I haven't..." Her words caught in her throat.

A tall, grungy, scruffy man who looked a lot like Jack stumbled out of the trees. He moved toward her, fist clenched and mumbling. "Like a tea tray in the sky, twinkle, twinkle little bat." Red blood streamed from his shimmering green eyes, taking Alice back to a time she'd rather forget, back to a guy with black-rimmed glasses standing over her with hate in his eyes and a virus in his veins, screaming at her.

Not again.

Chapter 3

Alice stared at him.

A grunt rolled out of his pale lips.

It's not real.

She tried to take a step away from him, but her feet ignored her. Alice's mind floated to that day in the theater, the smell of the campfire and smoke adding to her panic. *There had been smoke in the theater too.*

She tried to take a deep breath to ground herself to the here and now, but the memories kept coming: talking to her dad and brother that morning, arguing with her mom about moving to a place covered in snow for half the year, and wearing that stupid sundress in protest.

Kaleb's voice weaved through the memories. "Alice, look at me, please."

She was stuck. A red cape billowed on the movie screen above her. The smell of popcorn... *Everything smelled like popcorn and blood.*

"Alice!" Kaleb's voice broke through the blurred memories and mixed with the sound of her pounding heart.

She met Kaleb's eyes.

The heat of the warm setting sun let her know she wasn't trapped in that dark theater. *It's a memory.*

The man who had stumbled from the woods moved toward her. Warm tears streamed down her face. *This can't be happening. Not again. It was a freak accident.* Alice looked at the guy, his face covered in dark blood.

The guy in front of her had been infected with WonderLand; there was no other explanation.

Kaleb motioned for Alice to stay put. She shook her head. *Not happening.* Kaleb wanted her to stay where she was, in front of a crazed virus victim. *Was he insane?* She knew what could happen if she didn't take action, and by action, she meant hiding.

Alice stared into the blood-soaked eyes of the person in front of her. *Will he follow me, or is he too far gone?* A spark of the person he had once been was still there, fighting against the effects of the virus. She knew from experience what it was like, how hard he'd have to fight to break through it. She didn't think he could do it.

"Alice," Kaleb called to her again. She looked up at him, and a flash of teal moved behind him. It was Linc. *What is he doing?*

In an empty voice, the man in front of her sang, "Twinkle, twinkle, little bat."

Alice clapped her hands over her ears, not wanting to hear the rambling again. She knew she needed to move, but she was unable to stop her mind from traveling back to the theater, to the pink smoke–filled room, to people screaming, and to the all-consuming anger...

Anger that was burning its way up from her somewhere deep inside. Alice sank to the ground, her vision flickering, color draining from the world around her, a husk of a person singing a song about a bat while the virus threatened to take control.

Alice did the only thing she could think of to stop it. She counted. *One, two, three...*

There's nothing that can be done for him. He's gone. Twenty-five, twenty-six, twenty-seven, twenty-eight... Like my mom.

Warm hands pulled Alice to her feet, and a masculine voice murmured soft words into her ear. Not hearing the words, she fought against the voice, even when it pulled her close. Not until she smelled the musky scent around him did she stop fighting. She knew. It was Kaleb. Alice relaxed, letting him pull her away toward the fire and its warmth, keeping her eyes down and fixed on the trampled dirt. *Kaleb would take care of it.*

He helped her onto a wooden picnic bench as someone placed a thin blanket on her shoulders. Alice watched the fire nearby, repeating to herself the words that had become her mantra. *I'm safe.* She breathed in. *I'm fine.* She breathed out. Someone placed a hand on her chin, moving Alice's gaze upward.

"I'm fine," she said out loud.

Kaleb let his hand drop away from her face and pulled her in for a quick hug. "Sure, you are."

Alice rested her head on his shoulder, fighting back the memories of that day in the theater. *It's happening again.* Even if this outbreak was contained, there was no way Red Queen Inc. could hide her, not this time. She'd have to disappear, again. It was the only way to keep the people around her safe. If anyone ever found out she was infected and not immune like the doctors at Red Queen thought, she'd be nothing more than a test subject. *Dr. Turtle won't be able to protect me again.*

"I need to..." Kaleb motioned to his phone.

She nodded. "Of course."

He kissed the top of her head and stood up, calling Linc over. They had a short whispered conversation, and then Linc came over and sat on the bench next to her. Thankfully he didn't say anything. She wasn't ready to talk.

Alice watched Kaleb through the red-orange flames as he called out orders to the people around him.

"Search the woods. Make sure there aren't more."

Tom nodded and started toward the woods. Ryan studied Jack, who now lay face down in the dirt, while DeeDee yelled into her phone.

Alice wasn't sure how much time had passed before Kaleb came back to sit next to her. Her mind was caught in a cyclone of fear.

Kaleb pulled her against him, wrapping his warm arms around her. Alice had told him about her mom and the theater a few months ago after he found her curled in a ball in her closet. They'd gone to an event at the student center. *It was popcorn. The smell still gives me nightmares.* "It's happening again."

He exhaled with a loud sigh. "I don't—" His phone rang, cutting him off. Alice laid her head on his chest, listening to his heartbeat to keep her mind from going to the bad place.

She couldn't hear the person on the other line but assumed it was Kaleb's boss—the CEO of Red Queen Inc., Reid Redding. *DeeDee probably called her.* Even if the rumors were true about their falling out, there was no way DeeDee wouldn't tell her sister about another outbreak of WonderLand.

His voice rumbled through his chest. "Ma'am." He paused, listening to the woman on the other end. "That's right, fifteen."

Kaleb looked down at Alice. "Me, Tom, Linc, and Ryan." Kaleb brushed a stray hair from her face. "Yes, ma'am, boys' trip." He looked over to the tall blonde girl who was leaning against Tom's Jeep, texting. "DeeDee. She just showed up."

Reid's demanding silvery voice rose from the phone. "My sister was never there."

"Of course."

The call ended. Kaleb stared down at his phone for a minute. Alice saw something cross his face. Fear? Doubt? She wasn't sure.

A distinctive thumping of an incoming helicopter sounded in the distance. It must have pulled Kaleb from his thoughts because he pulled Alice to her feet. Their eyes met for a split second before he reached into his pocket.

"What's going on?" she asked.

Kaleb handed Alice the keys to his car. "Are you okay to drive?"

Her hands shook. She wasn't sure she could, but she nodded. "Kaleb, what's going on?" she asked again. "Why did you lie about my being here?"

He grabbed her hand, leading her to the car, DeeDee following close behind. "I'll explain..." The thumping got closer, cutting Kaleb off mid-sentence.

Instead of helping her into the driver's seat, he pushed Alice into the passenger seat. DeeDee slipped into the driver's seat. Kaleb stood next to DeeDee's open door, whispering something to her.

"Alice." He looked at her from the driver's-side door, shaking his head as if he were going to say something and changed his mind. "Make sure DeeDee doesn't hurt my baby," he half-heartedly joked as he stroked the hood of his car. "She's not used to unskilled drivers."

Alice knew if Kaleb was letting DeeDee drive his car, something really bad was happening. *If he could act like things were normal, so can I.* She smoothed her hand across the black dash of his beloved Camaro. "I won't let anything happen to your precious."

DeeDee's door slammed, and Kaleb moved around the car, standing far enough away that they could pull out. Alice turned and with shaking hands held the keys out to DeeDee. The soft white fur of the rabbit foot keychain skated Alice's fingertips as the keys fell into DeeDee's hand; a moment later, the engine roared to life.

Alice stared at the green tree air freshener that hung from the mirror, the memories creeping in around her again. The day had started with an argument.

Her mom's voice rang in her ears. "A sundress, really? Alice, it's thirty degrees outside."

Alice hadn't wanted to move. Her way of rebelling was to not change her wardrobe to adjust for the colder climate. It drove her mom crazy.

The image of her mom's lifeless eyes flashed across Alice's mind, the once white dress now blood-soaked, and the words "We have a survivor" echoed in her mind.

Alice shook her head, trying to forget, to leave the past in the past. But it wasn't the past, not if the virus had gotten out again. She needed a distraction. Alice reached out and pressed play on the old cassette player. *Hopefully, Kaleb has something decent to listen to.* The screeching voice of a band she had never heard of moved through the car, causing a sick pounding in her head. Alice pressed the eject button, and the cassette player spat out the old black tape.

"Maybe there's something on the radio." DeeDee reached over to switch to the radio, and static filled the car.

"I think we're still too far out to get anything."

The car fell silent again. Alice studied DeeDee, the girl she had met in the parking lot outside the theater. Alice hadn't spent much time with her since DeeDee had transferred to the university. They had a few classes together and even belonged to the same sorority, but Alice had done everything she could to avoid her.

"Rabbit seriously needs to update the sound system in this car," DeeDee said. "Who still has a tape player?"

Alice shrugged. "He feels like it would ruin her charm."

"Of course he does." DeeDee smiled.

It was the first genuine smile Alice had seen on DeeDee since the day they met. Back then, DeeDee seemed like she was so full of life, one of those people who made everyone feel welcome and special. The person in the driver's seat had lost that; she could be that person occasionally, but it seemed forced. There was a hint of sadness that pulsed from her, and for the first time, Alice wondered if DeeDee had lost someone that day too.

"So the virus, it wasn't a one-time thing, then?" Alice asked DeeDee.

DeeDee glanced over at her and sighed. "Alice, it never..."

Vworp! Vworp!

Alice looked down at her phone, expecting a text message. Instead, Kaleb's smiling face appeared on the screen, letting her know he was calling.

Kaleb started talking before she could even say hello. "Hey, wanted to check in and let you know that I won't be in class tomorrow, so take good notes. You're a doll." The phone disconnected. *That was it.*

Alice stared down at the phone, confused. There weren't any

classes tomorrow or for an entire week. "It sounded like he was leaving a voicemail," she said out loud.

"What did he say?" DeeDee asked.

She put the phone back in her pocket. "He asked me to take notes in class tomorrow and called me a doll."

DeeDee clenched the steering wheel. "Sorry, it was a message for me." She chewed on her cheek. "We can't let my sister know you were there today."

Alice was confused. She knew DeeDee and Ms. Redding—*Reid, she asked me to call her Reid*—had a falling out, but was it wise not to tell? The doctors at Red Queen would need to know she might have been exposed to the virus again. Dr. Turtle would need to know. He was the only one who knew she was infected. "Why?"

The click of the blinker filled the car, and DeeDee pulled to the side of the road. Alice turned to the back window, looking for the red and blue lights of a police car. It was the only reason she could think of for DeeDee to pull over. The road was empty. Confused, Alice turned to DeeDee, who had taken off her seat belt and was staring at Alice.

"Alice, I know you don't trust me."

Alice opened her mouth to tell DeeDee that it wasn't that she didn't trust her but that she wasn't sure how to be around her. She knew it wasn't fair to DeeDee, but she blamed her for what had happened in that theater. DeeDee put her hand up, stopping Alice from interrupting her. Alice was relieved. She wasn't ready to have that conversation.

"I wouldn't trust me after everything that has happened to you because of my family. You trust Kaleb, though."

Alice nodded. *What was she getting at?*

"And he trusts me."

Kaleb did trust DeeDee, though Alice wasn't sure why. According to Kaleb, they hadn't spoken much since they were kids, but they had a class together, and DeeDee didn't have many friends here, outside the sorority. So, he invited her to things hoping she could make a few friends and have a normal college experience.

DeeDee went on. "That message was letting me know he would be gone a few days and that we need to be vigilant. The people that work for my sister will be poking around. They can't know you knew anything about this. She is already too interested in you."

Alice's father had said something along the same lines after her mother had died, warning Alice against sharing too much with Reid Redding. Alice hadn't put much thought into it; she didn't share with anyone anyway, besides Kaleb, but even then, she kept things from him.

Sure, Red Queen helped her become anonymous again after the incident. They'd even paid her college tuition, though she had to agree to go into the lab once a week for tests. The doctors still couldn't understand how Alice hadn't lost her mind in the theater. She knew it was because of the anger management classes she'd taken after her parent's divorce. They'd kept the rage the virus invoked from overwhelming her senses.

Maybe DeeDee was right. Alice agreed.

DeeDee's shoulders sank with relief, and she smiled at Alice before putting her seat belt back on and getting on the road. A flash of bright white lightning streaked across the sky, followed by a loud crash of thunder. Alice would ask Kaleb when he got back what he thought about keeping her involvement a secret. She listened to the soft patter of rain on the steel roof, letting the peace of it wash over her. *Hopefully, he will be honest and not put his need to protect me above sharing.*

CHAPTER 4

Kaleb slid his phone into his jeans' pocket. He hoped Alice gave DeeDee the message. If not, he would have to find a different way to set up a meeting with the leader of the Task Force. Kaleb sighed. He knew he should have called DeeDee, but he needed to hear Alice's voice. To know she was okay.

The haunted look in her eyes when Jackson stumbled out of the woods babbling nonsense would be cemented in Kaleb's memories for the rest of his life.

Kaleb looked at the bag that held his classmate's body. *What will the story be this time? How will Red Queen ask me to cover this one up?*

Ryan approached Kaleb, that ever-present smile of his gone and replaced with a stern glare. Linc had brought Ryan into their circle a few months ago, stating they needed someone with ties to the government, someone who couldn't be bought. Kaleb wasn't sure about the "couldn't be bought." Something about the man bothered him. It was as if he were holding something back. The question was, how would he affect the mission?

Ryan's voice boomed over the incoming storm. "We've found twenty so far."

He watched the group of people in unneeded hazmat suits, the red heart insignia of Red Queen Inc. bright against the white of the suit, as they placed another body bag on the ground. *Thankfully the cloud that carried the virus had dissipated long before Alice and the others had gotten there.*

"Have you heard how the virus got out?" Ryan asked.

Kaleb shook his head. He didn't know but suspected that Reid Redding had something to do with it. Red Queen's cleanup crew got to the campsite in minutes instead of the hour it should have taken, almost as if they were on standby. *More of her unethical experiments.* Last time that had happened... He pushed the memory aside. He didn't have time to stew over his part in that. He wasn't that person anymore. The only reason he was still with Red Queen Inc. was to find a way to destroy Reid Redding and anyone who was there that day. It was the only way he knew to protect Alice.

Linc emerged from the wooded area, staring down at his tablet. He never looked up. Tom followed close behind, keeping his brother from tripping over rocks and other things. Watching them was strange. Tom would see an obstacle, and with a whisper or a whistle, he would let Linc know it was there. Kaleb wished he had that kind of relationship, or any relationship, with either of his brothers.

"The water," Linc muttered as he swiped at the raindrop that fell on the tablet.

The storm that had been threatening for the last hour started its descent. Kaleb scanned the area, making sure anything that could be damaged by water—lab equipment, paperwork—was covered. Ms. Redding would have his head if any of her "research" was ruined.

"What about the water?" Ryan asked.

Tom looked to Linc, who was lost in his research and ignoring the group. "Linc found traces of the WonderLand in the lake water," Tom answered.

Kaleb turned to Ryan. "It's the virus."

Ryan swore under his breath. "How does that even happen? I thought it was contained."

Kaleb eyed Linc and Tom. *Huh... That's interesting. The Sanchez brothers hadn't told him everything. Would experiments on unwilling "volunteers" be too much?*

Linc looked up, an answer on his lips, but he stopped midword to look over Kaleb's shoulder. "That was quick," he said.

Kaleb turned around. His father and Dr. Turtle stood next to a black van and a woman holding a large red umbrella overhead. The two men moved toward them. Marci, Ms. Redding's assistant and at the moment the umbrella holder, followed close behind. Kaleb looked for the CEO of Red Queen Inc., but she was nowhere to be found.

"Sir," Linc, Tom, and Ryan said in unison.

His father's stone figure loomed over him, waiting. Kaleb held back a grimace. He hated working with his father. After the theater and the part his father had played in destroying their once happy family, Kaleb would rather never see the man again. Instead, Kaleb not only still worked for him but had pulled more people into his destructive circle. *It's necessary,* he reminded himself. *It's the only way to help Alice. Ryan, Tom, and Linc know the risk of working for the Task Force and Red Queen Inc.*

Kaleb met his father's gaze and called him by his given name, knowing how much he hated it. "Joseph."

Annoyance darted across his father's face, but he said nothing. Satisfied he had gotten to his father even if it was for only a second, Kaleb smiled inwardly.

Joseph nodded toward the body bags. "How many?"

"Twenty," Ryan reported.

Dr. Turtle smirked. "That's..."

Kaleb glared at the little man, knowing how twistedly his mind worked. Those people had families and friends who cared about them, but to Turtle, they were lab rats.

Dr. Turtle looked down at his shoes, kicking at the ground, but he still had a twinkle of excitement in his eyes. "Horrible," Dr. Turtle stuttered.

Kaleb glanced over to Marci, trying to hold back a smart-mouth comment and disgust at Turtle's excitement. *Now's not the time.*

Marci closed the umbrella, shaking the water off. Kaleb looked up at the sound and was surprised she had guided them in her silent, almost invisible way to an overhanging tarp the cleanup crew had set up on their arrival. Fat drops of rain pounded above and around them, drowning out the possibility of a conversation. They watched the cleanup crew load the last of the bodies into the van, the rain washing away the evidence of what had happened.

Joseph moved closer to Kaleb, his eyes following each body bag to the van. "I count eighteen," he said.

"There are two who haven't succumbed to the virus." Ryan met Kaleb's eyes. "Yet?"

Kaleb nodded. He didn't want to give false hope. In all the tests, Alice had been the only person to survive the virus.

"They're only kids," Tom whispered next to him.

Linc and Kaleb exchanged a look. They had both seen the far-off gaze in Tom's eyes before, the one that meant Tom was holding on to the real world by his fingertips. The last time this happened, he disappeared for six months. Linc found him strung out on one of the designer drugs he had stolen from the labs at Red Queen Inc. Kaleb should have never helped Tom get his job back. Things were not going to get any better. Reid Redding had a lot of money and friends in high places; it was going to take more than a few "accidents" to stop her.

Kaleb hadn't realized how close Dr. Turtle had been following the conversation until his shrill voice screeched, the excited gleam back in his eyes. "Show me!" Turtle didn't care about the virus' most recent victims. He only cared about his research.

Kaleb had spent many hours in the doctor's lab watching his "experiments." The pain-filled screams of his "volunteers" echoing off the bright white walls of the lab were too much. Whenever Kaleb would say something, Joseph would remind him that this was the job. Besides, there was nothing that could be done. The people who came to Red Queen were usually volunteers, and those that weren't... Well, no one was looking for them.

His father had made sure Kaleb was in the room for the ones who didn't want to be there, helping to restrain them. It was his way of making sure Kaleb was compliant. This way, Kaleb would be guilty of the same atrocities as everyone else. *Joseph's insurance policy.* He had no idea that the moment Kaleb had walked back into his father's life, he had been working to bring down Red Queen Inc.

Linc led Dr. Turtle through the mud puddles left by the storm, which had ended. They stopped at the van that held the two surviving victims. Joseph stomped off in the opposite direction, Tom and Ryan following close behind. With nothing to be done, Kaleb pulled out his phone again and debated calling Alice. He knew DeeDee would take care of her. That was part of the deal. He worked for the Task Force gathering evidence against Red Queen Inc., and in return, the Task Force kept Alice safe.

A phone chirped behind him, and even though he knew it wasn't his, he looked at the dark screen of his phone before turning around. Marci sat perched on a large white cooler, looking down at her pink glitter phone. Kaleb had forgotten she was there. She was so quiet that her presence disappeared into the surroundings; that's what made her good at her job. Her fingers moved across the keypad, and a smile spread across her face, softening her features.

He knew that smile; it was the one she used when talking to her twin sister. The two women's personalities were at odds with each other. Kit was a ball of energy. Although a nice person, Kaleb found it draining to be around her. Unlike Marci, who was easy to talk to—when you knew she was in the room.

Marci didn't look up from her phone, but in a neutral voice she said, "I got that info on Ryan you wanted."

Kaleb had forgotten he had asked Marci to research Ryan for him. He could have done it himself, but Marci was faster. Kaleb's hacking skills were nothing compared to hers. Plus, she had contacts in the criminal underworld he could only imagine getting. That was the reason he had brought her into his spy network, along with Linc.

They worked with both the Task Force and Red Queen Inc. in an effort to shut down Ms. Redding's labs.

Three years ago Ms. Redding found out someone hacked into her system and took the footage from the theater. She was furious and demanded their death. One look at the hacker's work and Kaleb knew he had to find them. They could be the key to bringing down Red Queen and its crazed CEO. It took some time, but Kaleb found Marci at a local café. Actually, she'd found him.

Her intrusion into Red Queen hadn't been to gain information—it was because she was bored. Once she'd seen the footage from that day in the theater, though, she'd made it her mission to end Red Queen Inc. Kaleb was going to be Marci's in. The head of security's son was an easy mark. At least, that was what she thought. She was surprised when Kaleb recruited her to help him destroy Red Queen. Somehow, he still wasn't sure how he had convinced both Reid Redding and the Task Force to let him bring Marci in.

"Twelve years back, a senator's daughter went missing," she said without looking up from her phone. "Small town down south. Her name was Lily." Marci looked up from her phone and stared at him for a moment, looking for something. *Was that supposed to mean something to me?*

She shook her head, a sad, resigned look on her face. *Yep, I probably should have known who that was.*

"Lily and her brother had been walking home from school," she said, "down some rural country road. A black van pulled up, and two men jumped out, taking the girl. They found the boy still trying to catch the van, ten miles from where she was taken."

Kaleb didn't understand what this had to do with Ryan. "And?"

Marci started to type something into her phone. "Oh, I didn't tell you the girl's full name. Lily Fade-Dixon. Senator Dixon's daughter and—"

Kaleb interrupted. "And Ryan's sister."

That explained a few things, but not why Ryan took this job. It was an off-the-books investigation into Red Queen. No pay. No backup. No support. If things went sideways, Ryan, and Kaleb for that matter, could be charged. It was one of the reasons Kaleb had contacted his brother Markus, who worked for the FBI and confirmed Ryan was on extended leave. He'd also warned Kaleb the only reason someone would take on a double life without pay was if there were something personal in it.

Joseph and Ryan moved into the cover of the tarp. Marci stood up and slid her phone back into the front pocket of her black pants. Joseph barked out an order. "Pack it up. We're out in twenty."

Kaleb nodded at his father and started to gather up the little bit of camping gear that Linc and Tom had unloaded before he got to the campsite. He used the simple task to go over the events of the day in his head and the information Marci had given him.

He grabbed a camp chair and shoved it into its bag. *How will today change things?* There was a timeline to get information out of Red Queen Inc. *Will this push that up?* Kaleb swung the chair across his shoulder and bent down to grab the cooler Marci had been sitting on. Her dark hair fell across her face as she bent down to help, clasping one of the rope handles in her hand. They stood up together and walked to the white truck that Jackson had driven up earlier that day. The plastic scraped against the metal truck bed, making Kaleb's skin crawl.

Jackson's lifeless eyes flashed in his mind. *How am I going to do this? He was my friend. Can I lie about how he died?*

A warm hand settled on his wrist, pink nails shining against his suntanned skin. Marci looked back toward the other men. When she decided they were alone again, she lowered her voice. "The van that took Ryan's sister, Lily—it was one of Red Queen Inc.'s."

CHAPTER 5

K aleb stepped into the Red Queen Inc. elevator. The familiar smell of stale cigarettes and coffee hung in the air. He pressed the heart-shaped button next to the B for the bottom floor. A '90s pop song played in a muted tone overhead. *Alice loves this song.* It had been two weeks since the incident at the lake, and Kaleb hadn't contacted her. He told himself it was because he was busy.

Cover-ups take time.

There had been a lot of people at the lake, and a part of his job was to make sure no one found out what was going on at Red Queen Inc. The deaths at the lake had been made to look like accidents, but not just any kind. They had to be bad—no way to retrieve the body bad. There was a boat accident and a couple of fiery car accidents. And then there was Jackson. Right now, he was a missing person. Ms. Redding's words rang in Kaleb's head. *Camping alone can be dangerous.* In a week or two, parts of Jackson would be found half-eaten deep in the woods.

The lake had been tricky. It needed to be closed to the public but not to the scientists from Red Queen Inc. Tom had suggested that a parasite could be found by one of their employees or interns while on vacation. Tom had pointed out it would explain the comings and goings of the Red Queen scientists. Plus, they could treat the lake free of charge, helping the near-bankrupt city clean up the mess.

Redding had loved the idea, and Kaleb had to admit it was a good one. Clean up the mess that Red Queen Inc. had created and get a tax write-off. It was evil, but genius.

The elevator dinged a floor above his stop, and the doors opened as a man with bright red hair stepped in. He was one of the interns who worked in the labs in the lower levels of Red Queen Inc. He fidgeted with his phone and avoided Kaleb's gaze. There was something about the kid that seemed familiar beyond working at Red Queen. Kaleb tried to remember his name. It was there on the edge of his mind, but all he could remember about him was that he had a class with Alice and was always trying to get her attention.

Alice... I have to call her today. She's probably worried sick. Normally they spoke every day, but neither of them had contacted each other since the lake—his idea. He'd been avoiding calling her. *I need to find a way to explain what happened at the lake without freaking her out.*

DeeDee and Marci had kept an eye on Alice for the last two weeks. Looking for changes, in case of infection—at least that was what DeeDee was looking for. Marci, on the other hand, was worried about her well-being. It was one reason why Kaleb had Marci placed as one of Alice's roommates, to watch over her. The incident at the lake must have brought up all kinds of horrible memories for Alice. It had for him, and he was only a spectator the first time around. *Besides, she's immune to the virus.*

The metal doors of the elevator slid open with a ding on the bottom floor; the red-haired guy rushed out the doors, bumping into Kaleb and mumbling an apology as he shuffled down a long white hall, disappearing from Kaleb's view.

"What was he in a rush for?" Kaleb asked himself, before realizing it was Friday. Kaleb looked down at his watch. 3:15. Alice's weekly appointment. *Shawn. That was his name. He must be trying to see Alice.*

Kaleb knew DeeDee had told Alice to avoid Red Queen until she had heard from him, but a part of him still hoped to catch a glimpse of Alice. Kaleb moved into the open waiting area. Cushioned chairs and cheap end tables covered in outdated magazines lined the walls. He walked across the room to the security desk to be buzzed through the heavy double doors. Eric Madison, one of the two security guards, stood to greet him, keeping his eyes on the college student who sat in the corner thumbing through an old fashion magazine, longingly looking at her phone every few minutes. Kaleb had seen that look many times in this waiting room. Phones didn't work down here. No signal. Nothing to look through except for ten-year-old magazines. He always wondered if it was some sort of torture.

"Your girl called—she's sick," Madison said.

Everyone had gotten into the habit of calling Alice Kaleb's girl. At first, he would argue it. *She could never feel like that about me. Not if she knew what I'd done.* Now he accepted it. Kaleb nodded as if he already knew that Alice was sick, happy that she had followed DeeDee's instructions and avoided Red Queen Inc. He motioned toward the girl in the corner. "New victim?"

"Rabbit, we are supposed to call them 'volunteers,'" Harrison, the other guard, air quoted.

Kaleb had "volunteered" once. It was the worst two hours of his life; having your emotions work against you sucked. He looked back at the girl. At least she would get paid. Hopefully, she didn't become a junky like so many who had tried the drugs Dr. Turtle's lab turned out. He doubted it, though; it was rare that anyone walked away from Red Queen alive.

He rolled his eyes at the security guards. "Yeah, she's a volunteer, for now."

"That's a bit heartless," Madison grumbled.

Kaleb shrugged. "Maybe. But it's the truth." If he could, he would grab the girl's arm and drag her far from this place. But it wasn't possible. Not if he wanted to succeed. He had to play the part: angst-ridden boss's son—well, almost-boss'. "Buzz me in."

Harrison pressed down on the large red button on the desk. The double doors opened into the area set up to look like an ER, and the smell of antiseptic and vomit overwhelmed his senses for a moment. People in white coats bustled around the bright white room looking busy.

He moved through the room, trying not to peek into the curtained-off rooms. It was easier if he didn't put a face to the volunteers. He kept his eyes down, fixed on the floor until he got to the maze of hallways in the back.

Kaleb remembered the first time he had come to the basement. He'd gotten lost and walked the halls for hours, with people buzzing past him, ignoring him. It was frustrating. Kaleb learned later it was normal to find drugged-out volunteers wandering through the hall. It was policy to ignore them. There were enough security cameras in the building that it was nearly impossible not to have someone watching you at all times, and Dr. Turtle or one of his interns would find them, eventually.

He stopped outside the twin doors of the conference room and stared at the large heart painted on the door. Taking a deep breath of the recycled air, he stepped into the crowded conference room. He was late and last to arrive like he'd planned. He had to keep up appearances. Joseph was the only one to make a note of his late arrival, looking down at his watch and back at Kaleb as he slid into the only available chair, a black cushioned thing next to Ryan.

Static crackled from the phone in the center of the long oval table. Ms. Redding's silvery voice flowed through the room, and Kaleb pretended to pay attention to the meeting that should have been an email.

Before hanging up, Ms. Redding said, "We are a family here, and we protect our own."

Joseph stood up at the head of the table next to Ms. Redding's empty monstrous chair and started lecturing. Kaleb tuned him out. Instead, he tried to compose the perfect text to Alice, deciding he would contact her as soon as he left the building. He wrote on a small scrap of paper.

Alice, I'm sorry I haven't called. *Nope.*

Alice, let's meet up for ice cream. *Really, ice cream? What is it, 1950?*

Doctor Who? *Arg. Why is this so hard?*

Kaleb wasn't sure how long he had been working on the message, but the meeting had ended, and he hadn't heard a word of it. The people around him rushed out of the room to complete whatever mundane assignment they'd been given.

He crumpled the paper he'd been writing on into a ball, shoved it into his pocket, and leaned back in his chair, pulling his fingers through his hair. He still had no idea what he was going to say to Alice. Everything he came up with sounded lame.

A small scrap of crumpled white paper fell from Ryan's notebook onto Kaleb's lap as he got up to leave. Ryan leaned down to pick up something from the floor. "Read it," he said in a whisper.

Kaleb uncrumpled the paper and read, **Get your girl out**. Confused, he handed the paper back to Ryan, meeting his dark, horror-stricken eyes. *What had I missed?* Before he could ask, Ryan shoved the crumpled paper into his notebook and rushed out the door.

KALEB HURRIED home after the meeting, but now he paced back and forth in his room, Ryan's note blazing in his memory. He had told Kaleb to get Alice out, but he hadn't given any other information. *Should I trust Ryan?* Kaleb sat down on his freshly made bed, his open laptop sliding into his thigh. Ryan had his own objectives—they all did. The real question was, did those objectives interfere with Kaleb's plans? Nothing Ryan had done made Kaleb think he would interfere. He'd done the job and reported everything to the Task Force. *Can I risk not trusting him?* He didn't think so. Not with Alice's life hanging in the balance. *I have to get Alice as far from here as possible.*

He pulled an envelope from a drawer, the paper crinkling in his hands. The green card plan was supposed to be a last resort, life or death. Kaleb wasn't sure if this was life or death, but it sure felt like it. He looked down at the card. It was instructions, coordinates, for Alice. It would guide her to their meeting place, somewhere to start their new lives. They'd find a small town or maybe a large city they could disappear in until the Task Force could bring down Red Queen Inc. and he could finally tell her everything. Not just the basic stuff, but everything.

This was what he wanted from the start, but DeeDee didn't think they could bring the wrongdoings of Red Queen to light without him. *If Alice is in danger, my agreement with DeeDee is over, and I'm free to go.* The heaviness in his chest lightened at the thought of being able to share everything with Alice, to get her away from Red Queen, Reid Redding, and his father.

Kaleb opened his bedroom door and stepped into the hallway, tucking the envelope with the green card inside into his back pocket. The sooner he got to Alice, the sooner they could start their new life.

He moved through the house he shared with Linc and Tom. It was cleaner than the house he had grown up in; Linc was a bit of a neat freak. He would miss that. He'd miss a lot of things, but Alice had always been his priority, since that day in the theater when he first saw her.

Sure, disappearing would be hard at first, and Alice might hate him after he told her about his part in everything. No, he couldn't think like that. Alice would forgive him. She would understand that he didn't know what was going to happen.

Kaleb got into his car and drove the short distance to Alice's place, texting Marci before starting the car. The green card plan had been Marci's idea. After Kaleb had shared with her what he was trying to do, he knew they needed a way out. He was good with computers, but Marci was a genius. She would also be the person that Red Queen and the Task Force would use to find Alice after they disappeared; it was perfect since Marci's loyalty lay with neither group but with Kaleb himself.

Marci paced outside the main door of her apartment, mumbling something under her breath. He'd never seen her like this; Marci kept her emotions to herself. It took a few seconds for her to even notice Kaleb was standing there. A wisp of doubt crept into his excitement. Marci stopped pacing, and Kaleb met her pale eyes, her emotions swirling around them. He tried to figure out what was going on, but Marci looked down at his shoes and took a deep breath. When she met his eyes again, the emotions that had swirled in her eyes moments before were now hidden behind a wall. *Not good.*

"You can't go," she blurted out.

Kaleb's stomach dropped. "What? Why?"

Marci toyed with the gold compass she wore around her neck. "Joe came to Reid's office today. He knows." Kaleb must have looked at her weird because Marci sped on. "He told Reid you were going to run. That you had been hostile."

"That's not new. I'm always hostile," Kaleb muttered.

She waved away his comment. "Alice still needs to go, but you can't go with her."

"Marci," he growled as the light feeling in his chest sank.

"Somehow they know. Reid and Joe found out that Alice was at the lake. Reid is demanding that Alice be brought in. At all costs."

"Who's bringing her in?"

"Tom."

The light feeling in his chest popped, leaving cement that settled in his stomach. "Tom? He's one of us." Okay, he had done some horrible things in his past. That was before Linc helped him get clean. *There has to be more to it.* Kaleb reassured himself before he remembered Linc expressing concern over Tom's actions since the incident at the lake. He'd been secretive, and Linc thought he might be using drugs again.

Kaleb could tell Marci was holding something back. He wondered if she would know whether Tom was using again.

Before he could ask any more questions, Kit's shrill voice echoed in the hallway behind them. She bounced toward them, her long hair swishing with each step. "OMG, Kaleb." She turned to her sister. "Why didn't you tell me Kaleb was here?"

On a normal day, Kaleb would have found Kit's childlike demeanor entertaining and refreshing considering what she had been like when he first met her. That jerk of an ex had left her a heap of a person, lost to the world. Now she was bubbly and book smart.

Kaleb looked down at his watch and back up at Kit. He didn't have time for her exuberance.

He hated to admit it, but Marci was right. Alice couldn't stay, and he couldn't go. Not if he wanted to keep her safe.

He sighed. Alice would be home soon, and he needed to disappear before she got there. If he saw her, he wouldn't be able to do what needed to be done. "Kit, do you have a green index card?" he asked. "And a sharpie?"

"Of course." She opened her backpack and pulled out a stack of fluorescent index cards. He pulled out a green card. EL 2020 was written in small white letters on the top right corner. Kit dug through her bag for a minute more before pulling out a box of pens, fanning them out for Kaleb, smiling. "Pick one."

He took the only black sharpie from her and pulled from his back pocket the white envelope that had given him hope of a new life moments before. Kaleb walked across the dry grass to use the nearby wall as a desk, the brown tips of the grass crunching under his feet. The red brick was warm from the sun; he moved closer to its heat, using his body to hide the new message. One word was all he wrote— RUN—and then he took out the old card and slid the new card into the envelope. *This way if I'm caught, I can't tell them where she is.*

"Can you get this to Alice?" He handed the envelope to Marci.

Marci took it from him without meeting his eyes. "Of course."

Kaleb started back to his car. A thought crossed his mind. *What if Alice doesn't take the note for what it is? What if she thinks it's a joke?* He needed to do something to show her the importance of following his instructions. "Wait." Kaleb held out his hand for the envelope, and Marci handed it to him. Pity or maybe sadness lined her face. Kaleb ignored it.

He grabbed his car key and lucky rabbit's foot—a gift from his mom—from his pocket. He held them for a minute, letting the memories of his life before Red Queen, when his mom was still around and they were a happy family, fill him. He had hoped to find a way to have that again one day. Maybe even with Alice. Now he'd be lucky if he ever saw her again.

He let the key tumble from his hands into the white envelope. *At least she'll have something to remember me by.*

CHAPTER 6

A lice pulled her phone from her bright green backpack as she descended the zigzag concrete stairs. It had been two weeks, and she still hadn't heard from Kaleb, and now DeeDee had disappeared. Alice sighed. She didn't know what to do. The people from Red Queen Inc. had called three times this week. She'd told them she'd been sick, but that excuse could only last for so long. The radio silence was driving her mad, causing her mind to go to horrible and irrational places.

These thoughts caused her vision to flicker on the edges, and Alice took a deep breath. *Kaleb will call; he's been busy, that's all. Still.* She typed in her phone the words **Where are you?** and then pocketed the phone without hitting send. She walked back to her apartment, taking the long way through the student center.

Kaleb would call her; he had never let her down. Granted, nothing like this had happened before. Sure, he was her best friend, but a person could only take so much. It was why she'd changed her name and stopped talking to her family. The incident at the theater had taken its toll on her father and brothers. When Reid and Dr. Turtle mentioned they could help her disappear, Alice had taken them up on their offer, feeling it would be better for everyone involved. *It's better to miss them than put them in danger.*

Music blared from the top floor of the three-story apartment she shared. Alice walked up the stairs to her dorm where the door to the community kitchen was open, and Kit and Marci sat at the table. Books and note cards still covered every inch of available space, the kitchen sink overflowed with unwashed dishes, and trash littered the floor. Alice stood in the doorway, wondering whose turn it was to do the dishes, not that it mattered; she knew she'd be the one to do them.

Looking up from her organic chem book, Kit said, "Hey." She turned down the music. "Kaleb stopped by."

"When?!"

Marci answered without looking up from her keyboard. "Maybe twenty minutes ago."

"No, more like an hour," Kit said.

"You have no concept of time, little sister. It was twenty minutes."

"You are only two minutes older, and I know exactly what time it was because—"

Alice interrupted the sisters before the argument got to the point that no one would be able to. "What did he say?"

Marci motioned toward the hall that held the bedrooms. "That he was on his way out of town, but he left something for you. I put it in your room."

Alice rushed out of the kitchen to her bedroom. In the center of her unmade bed was an envelope with her name scrawled across it in Kaleb's perfect handwriting. She had always teased him about the flowery curves of his letters, but secretly she loved the way the letters danced on the page. Alice picked up the envelope, hoping it had some answers.

The weight of it let her know there was more than a piece of paper inside. Alice slid a finger under the seal, the tearing paper echoing in her ears. A bright green index card peeked out from the white confines. *Something happened*, she thought.

In the center of the card was one word written in bold, bumpy black letters.

RUN.

It has to be a joke. There has to be more.

Alice tipped the envelope over in her lap; a single key attached to a white rabbit's foot fell out. The key had a black plastic covering with the cross-like Chevy emblem stamped on it. *Dorothy.* Kaleb had given her the key to his car and told her to run? Alice turned the card over in her hand, looking for more. Instructions on where they should meet, anything. The green card was a last resort, a way to keep them safe if anything went south.

What changed?

She opened her closet and pulled out an old duffel bag. She knew Kaleb was playing a dangerous game, and her involvement with him put her at risk. She opened the top drawer of her dresser, throwing socks and underwear into the bag. There should have been instructions on where they would meet. *Could he have left them in the car?* Alice asked herself. *No, if he left the keys to Dorothy, it means he is not coming.* She pulled an old faded pair of blue jeans and her university sweatshirt from the laundry and shoved them into the bag.

Alice sat down on her bed, trying to remember where she had left her favorite shoes. Closing her eyes, she tried to visualize the last time she had seen them. It wasn't her sneakers' location but Jack's shimmering green eyes calling to her, blood washing away the person he once was.

Alice's heart sped up as her grip on reality started to slip. *One—* she took a deep breath—*two, three, four...fifteen.* Alice opened her eyes and looked around her room. It was in color, nothing red and bright calling to her, begging her to hurt someone.

She thought about her life since the theater, how she had been content to sit on the sidelines, letting Kaleb take the risk all in an effort to find out what happened that day in the theater.

How long before he was infected? She thought about the lake. *Would it have happened if I had spoken out all those years ago?*

Alice walked through her room, shoving things into her bag. *I'm responsible for what happened at the lake, maybe not directly, but I didn't say anything after that day in the theater. I let Reid Redding help me disappear.*

She picked up the green card. "This is ridiculous." *Where am I going to go?* She couldn't go home to her father; that would put her family in danger. *How long before I lose control and hurt them?* Her brothers knew how to press her buttons like little brothers do. *Besides, it would be the first place Red Queen would look for me.*

He could've at least left instructions on where to go. It's not like last time I disappeared. I had help then.

She stood in the center of her room, looking at the framed photos on the shelf above her bed. Kaleb dressed as a mobster to her flapper. Marci and Kit with her at a Halloween party and Tom throwing Linc into a pool fully clothed. *How am I going to do this?*

"Damn him." Alice tossed the duffel bag across the room. It made a satisfying crunch as it crashed into the wall. She grabbed her phone and dialed Kaleb's number. *No answer. Of course.* Dropping her phone on the bed, she debated her best course of action.

She could run like Kaleb asked, with no direction, funds, or way to contact anyone. *What kind of life would I have? How long can I live like that? How long before Red Queen finds me?*

Before she ran, she needed to try to talk to Kaleb. *Maybe if I'm careful, I can get to him without causing any trouble. Find a way to communicate while I'm on the run.* She knew it was a stupid idea, but she had to try.

Grabbing Kaleb's key, she walked out the door, leaving her half-packed duffel bag and cell phone on the bed. Kit and Marci were still in the kitchen studying and didn't look up as she passed by. Alice looked for Kaleb's car in the parking lot and started toward it, anger growing inside with each step. Thinking better of it, Alice decided walking to his house would be a better idea. It would help burn off some of her frustration.

Alice walked up the concrete steps to the front door of the house Kaleb shared with Tom and Linc, lost in her thoughts. It wasn't until she stood at the door that she noticed it was open, not in the someone-forgot-to-close-it way, but in a broken remnant that might have once been a door. She looked past it into the living room. The place was trashed. Not the crazy-party kind of trashed, but a drug-dealer-looking-for-someone's-stash kind of trashed.

The couch cushions were ripped to shreds. The coffee table lay on its side in the center of the room. The curtains Alice had made, a housewarming gift, were crumpled on the dirt-covered carpet. She wiped her hands on her skirt.

Do I go in? Or try to find help? Of course, get help.

Alice reached into her back pocket to grab her phone, but it wasn't there. She'd left the phone on her bed. *Now what? I could use a neighbor's phone.*

She peered around the door to the next house over. *No cars in the driveway, meaning no one home. Now what? Maybe go back to the school. Surely someone will have a phone there.*

A loud crash came from somewhere in the back of the house, and she thought she heard Linc scream, and even though she knew it was a bad idea, she went in. *This is how people get killed,* she told herself.

Unlike the stupid girls in the movies, she didn't go rushing toward the noise. Instead, she moved through the house with as much stealth as a five-foot something woman could in a demolished bachelor pad. The noise had come from one of the back rooms that belonged to Linc and Tom. She'd seen the Jeep outside and worried that one of them might be hurt.

Alice made her way to the kitchen, avoiding broken glass and shards of ceramic scattered on the laminate floor as she walked. The small dark oak kitchen table was tipped upside down, and the two matching chairs were tossed into the doorway, blocking the way to the backyard. *Had the chairs landed that way, or had someone blocked the only other exit on purpose?*

Her foot landed on a clear piece of broken glass, the sound of its crunching a drum announcing her arrival. She paused, making sure that no one knew she was there. The only noise was coming from the back rooms.

She didn't think anyone heard her and kept moving toward the back of the house, listening for the intruder with every step. It was as if it had taken half a lifetime to get through the kitchen, but when Alice's sneakered foot stepped on the squishy brown carpet in the hall, she held back a sigh of relief. The plush carpet would hide her footfalls better than the kitchen floor.

Alice listened for any signs of danger. A familiar voice drifted through the hall from the room up ahead of her. She took a few steps toward the door to listen. Two male voices argued through the door of the bedroom next to Kaleb's, a room they used as a sort of office and game room.

"You had one job."

Kaleb's voice boomed down the hall. "Alice has nothing to do with this."

"You will bring her in," Ryan said.

Alice swallowed the bitter taste of fear that tried to escape her throat. *Bring me in?* She had no idea who Ryan worked for, only that he gave her the creeps. *Kaleb was right; I should have run.* That was what she was going to do. Alice turned around, intending to go out the way she came, but something moved across her vision, a shadow of a person. She wasn't sure who it was, but after what she'd heard, it was best if they didn't see her. Alice ducked into the room closest to her, Kaleb's bedroom.

Unlike the rest of the house, the room was spotless, not a single thing out of place. The bed was even made. Alice sat down on Kaleb's bed, his open laptop bumping her leg, and she pushed it away. The screen came to life, a video he had been watching frozen. It was the theater, the one that her mother had died in.

Alice picked up the laptop. The date stamp on the right corner glowed orange. It was two weeks before her mother had died. A boy with blond curls stood in front of the double doors that lead into the large screening room. *Is that Kaleb?*

She didn't want to believe it. He'd told her he worked for Red Queen back then, but he spent most of his time behind a computer.

Alice's finger hovered over the play button. She wanted to find out what Kaleb was doing, why he was at that theater two weeks before the incident.

The voices in the next room stopped, and their heavy steps sounded outside the door. She needed to hide. *I'll have to ask him later.*

Alice scanned her surroundings, looking for somewhere she would go unnoticed and cursing herself again for not leaving when she had the chance.

There were two choices of hiding places and neither of them good. Under the bed or in the closet. Alice pulled the slatted folding doors of the closet closed at the same time as the bedroom door burst open. She made herself as small as possible, curling into a ball in the back corner, behind a pair of pants.

"No one is in here," Kaleb said.

A dark shadow moved in front of the door. "I heard something."

"Linc is back at base, and no one else would have a reason to be here." She heard the bed squeak under Kaleb's weight. "Let's just finish. You get the bathroom, and I'll start here."

Ryan leaned against the closet door, and it creaked in protest. "Bathrooms are done."

Alice pushed further back into the corner of the closet. *What's going to happen if they find me?* The doors slid open a crack. Alice bit her cheek, holding back a scream. She knew deep down if they found her, Kaleb wouldn't be able to help her. The door opened a little more, and Alice's vision flickered into black and white.

Not now.

"I'll get the bed," Kaleb said.

Good. That meant Ryan would be the one to get this side of the room. It made things easier if it was Ryan she had to attack. She moved her hands across the thick carpet looking for something to use as a weapon, looking for the red color the virus would highlight as a weapon.

The doors opened with a clack and squeal. Something flashed not quite red but pink next to her. Alice grabbed at it and ran toward Ryan with a steel-toed boot in her right hand. Not the best weapon, but it was the only thing she could find. She hoped it would surprise him.

Ryan's foot moved under her, and Alice fell face-first onto the gray carpet at the same moment Kaleb screamed her name.

Alice rolled onto her back, her breath coming in short spurts. She concentrated on the white speckled ceiling, trying to gain control. Both men were on her, holding her down. Alice kicked at them. Ryan dodged her leg and then moved to sit on her flailing limbs. She tried to scream. A hand covered her mouth.

Ryan glared at Kaleb. "No one is here, huh? So that's why you couldn't find her, because you were hiding her."

Kaleb's eyes met Alice's with an unsaid apology before looking to Ryan. "I didn't know she was here. Her roommates said she was leaving after her last class. She was going to visit some family."

He was lying. Alice didn't speak to her family. Plus he'd left her that note. Kaleb had tried to protect her, and she hadn't listened. *I should have run.*

Ryan motioned with his jaw toward Kaleb's pocket. "Give it to me."

Kaleb shook his head. "We don't need to. She'll come with us." He looked at Alice, trying to communicate something to her. "Won't you?"

She nodded.

Of course she would go with them. She trusted him. Kaleb wouldn't knowingly hurt her. He had to have a plan; why else would he deliberately lie to Ryan?

"You know that's not what Ms. Redding wants."

Ryan put his knee in the center of Alice's chest. She held back a groan, not wanting him to know he had hurt her. Ryan reached into Kaleb's back pocket and pulled out a large syringe.

Alice's eyes widened at the sight of the swirling green liquid in the cylinder. She bit down on her tongue.

Drops of green slid down the thin metal of the needle.

The temperature in the room seemed to rise, and waves of heat swam around Alice. Her lunch moved from her stomach to her throat, and a cold sweat spread across her face.

Alice would do whatever they wanted if it meant not having some unknown substance injected into her veins.

She closed her eyes, fighting the darkness that pulled at her, fighting the fear of not knowing what was in the syringe. What would it do to her?

The prick of a needle entered her arm and forced Alice to open her eyes. Ryan was staring down at her, a look of hatred or pity plastered on his face. She turned away from him and the needle he held in his hand, not wanting to see either.

The cold green fluid moved through her arm, pulling her thoughts from the rational until her brain simmered in a stew of fear, action twitching in her veins.

CHAPTER 7

Kaleb hit his bedroom floor, hard, Alice's elbow slamming into his side moments before their eyes met. The fear he saw there was unnatural. He reached out to her, trying to stop her, but she fled.

"Damn." He pushed himself to his feet. *Ryan had done it. He'd actually given her the Timore, and it worked. It shouldn't have worked. Why had it worked?* Kaleb ran through the house he'd helped trash, avoiding the broken pieces of his soon-to-be former life, the front door in his sight.

The bright sun bounced off Alice's dark hair as she exited, the door slamming behind her.

Tom, who had been lurking around the house since Kaleb came back from Alice's earlier, stepped out of the shadows, blocking Kaleb's pursuit.

"What the hell are you doing?" Kaleb shouted.

Tom looked up at him, his eyes glazed over from whatever drug was running through his system. "We expected this," he said.

"We who?"

Ryan came up behind Kaleb. "Redding."

Kaleb turned to face Ryan, who wouldn't make eye contact.

Ryan went on. "She thinks Turtle's keeping something from her. Something to do with Alice."

Of course he is, but there has to be a better way than drugging Alice.

Kaleb looked at Tom, who was still blocking the door. "I don't have time for this."

"Alice is fine," Tom croaked. "We have someone following her. I'm sure they will pick her up soon."

"You *what?*" Kaleb screamed moments before his fist connected to the clammy soft skin of Tom's face.

Tom crumbled to the floor, rubbing his jaw. "I thought you knew."

Kaleb turned around, pushing Ryan out of his way, going back to his bedroom. He needed to get her back and away from Red Queen, and there was only one way he could think of doing that: with the flash drive he'd stolen from Turtle months ago.

He opened the top drawer of his dresser and pulled out a small penknife before going to one of the closet doors. It wasn't the best hiding spot, but it was the only place he could think of that his father or one of the goons wouldn't think to look. Kaleb moved the knife across the bottom edge of the closet door, forcing the peg holding it together to come loose. A small black flash drive fell to the floor. Kaleb slid it into his pocket as Ryan stormed into the room.

"They don't have her."

Kaleb stood up. "What? How?"

"Red Queen, they don't have Alice."

Kaleb's stomach dropped. "Where is she?"

"Nobody knows. They were supposed to grab her the second she left here. Had a van outside waiting and everything. She got past them." Ryan looked behind him, then back at Kaleb, dropping his voice so Tom couldn't hear. "Just go."

Still putting on a show for Tom, Ryan called over his shoulder. "We have to bring you in." He motioned to the window, dropping his voice again. "Go out the window."

Confused, Kaleb looked at Ryan and mouthed, "What's going on?"

Ryan shook his head and pointed to the window, mouthing back, "Now."

Kaleb didn't need to be told twice. Okay, maybe he did.

He stood up on the desk that sat under the window, popped out the screen, and climbed through it. He landed on the wet grass and ran toward campus, past the van that was parked in front of their house.

He'd made it as far as the creepy rotunda Alice loved when his phone buzzed with an incoming call from DeeDee. He hit ignore. He didn't have time to deal with whatever emergency she had.

Kaleb looked inside the rotunda, a part of him hoping Alice had hidden away among the statues and yet another part relieved at the same time that she hadn't. His phone rang again. He pulled it out of his pocket to see DeeDee's smiling face looking up at him.

Confident no one had followed him and needing a minute to think, Kaleb leaned against one of the statues that formed a circle and answered his phone.

"What?"

DeeDee's panicked voice rang in his ears. "Have you found Alice yet?"

"How do you know she's missing?"

"Reid." DeeDee sighed. "She just called me wondering if I knew where she was. I don't know what my sister is up to, but you can't let her find Alice. Take Alice and go somewhere that's not here. The safe house in Salt City, you both should be safe there." And without a goodbye, DeeDee hung up.

So, Ms. Redding told DeeDee Alice was missing. Ms. Redding must be frantic, but what does she want with Alice?

Kaleb scrolled through his phone. He needed help, there were too many places to look and not enough time. First, he called Marci, who was already out looking for Alice, followed by Linc. They agreed to call him first if either of them found her.

He considered going back to Alice's place and getting his car, but he didn't have time to find the keys, if she had even left them there, so he jogged toward the only other place on campus he was sure she'd go.

He'd almost made it to the top of the zigzag stairs that separated the two main parts of campus when his phone rang incoming video chat. Kaleb pulled the phone out of his back pocket. Linc stared up at him from the screen.

"Found her." Linc turned the screen, focusing on a woman curled up asleep on a brick floor.

"Where?"

Linc's face came back on screen. "The creepy statue thing near the house."

She wasn't there fifteen minutes ago. How had I missed her?

A text message came up on the screen from Marci.

Linc let me know he found Alice.

I'm just up the street, near the science building.

Can be there in five.

Kaleb walked past the science building toward the street and sent a text back.

I'm on the corner. Pick me up on your way.

Marci's blue sedan pulled up next to him at the same time he hung up with Linc, who'd agreed to stay put and not wake Alice. Kaleb opened the door and climbed into the front seat without a word.

Neither of them spoke as she drove down the hill toward Alice, the only sound the light rain tinkling on the glass windshield.

Marci parked the car near the rotunda. Before unlocking the door, she handed Kaleb a bottle of water with the Red Queen logo. "Stole it from Reid's office. It should help."

He watched Marci step out of the car, leaving him wondering if this was the counter to the Timore. There were rumors that Reid had a remedy for everything that came into or left Red Queen—well, everything but WonderLand.

They walked through the rain and met Linc near one of the statues. "How much did you give her?" Linc asked.

Marci's phone rang. "Sorry. I have to take this," she said as she walked back to her car.

Kaleb grumbled, "I have no idea. Ryan's the one who gave it to her."

"Tom was there, wasn't he."

Should I tell him?

Linc said. "And he's using again."

"You know?"

Linc frowned. "It started right after the lake, and since then he's done some terrible things, so Gryff and his Knights keep the drugs coming."

Marci came back as the rain started to clear. "Look, I have to go, but before I do, I was thinking that if the Timore is still in Alice's system when she wakes up, it might be a good idea if Linc is the one to talk to her."

Kaleb interrupted. "I don't know if that's a good idea."

"She cares about you, trusts you. If she's affected by the drug, then she's going to run, and we might not be the ones to find her next."

She is right, of course.

Marci went on. "Linc's more of a friend of a friend. She doesn't know him that well and shouldn't have any strong emotions toward him, making it less likely she'll take off again. At least I think that's how she feels about him."

Kaleb handed Linc the bottle of water. "Leave it where she can see it when she wakes up. I'll stand back out of sight until we know if the Timore is still in her system."

Linc nodded before heading further into the rotunda.

Once he was out of sight, Marci spoke. "I'm heading out of town. Kit's ex showed up at the apartment, and she's completely freaked. She's taking off. I suggest you do the same."

Kaleb nodded but didn't say anything. He would get Alice to safety even if that meant staying behind to do it. Kaleb put his hands in his pocket. "Call if you need anything."

Marci turned to go, but before she got too far, Kaleb remembered the flash drive and called out to her. Pulling the sleek black rectangle out his pocket, he handed it to Marci. "I'm not sure what's on this, but I know it's important to Turtle. Keep it safe."

CHAPTER 8

Cold surrounded Alice. It crept into the depths of her body, causing the bones in her arms and legs to scream out in agony. She tried to move, but a deep pain vibrated through her. A moan escaped her dry throat. *What happened?* Alice reached for the cup of water she kept on her nightstand. It wasn't there. Neither was her nightstand.

I must have fallen asleep on the couch again.

Alice tried to force her sleepy eyes open, but they refused. She lay there listening to the quiet that filled the room, the smell of fresh rain and wet concrete floating in the air around her.

She was sure Kit left the window open again. *Grr.* She thought about the mess that would have to be cleaned up. Last time, one of Alice's favorite books had been ruined by the rainwater. She forced her eyes open, knowing the longer the water sat, the worse the damage would be.

A bright light from the sun peeked through the clouds and burned her tired eyes. A sharp pain shot through her arm as she moved it to shield her face, angry-looking square-shaped lines marking the skin of her arm. Sleeping on the couch usually resulted in aches and pains in weird places, but this one was a bit different.

She scanned her surroundings, expecting to see puddles on the carpet and ruined books, not a concrete bench. *Where am I?*

Alice stared down at the bricks, letting her fingers trace one of the names etched into the stone below. E-l-i-z-a M-o-r-r-i-l-l. It was her mother's name, put here when she'd been a student, long before her mother had met Alice's dad and had kids.

She rolled into a sitting position, her eyes adjusted to the sunlight. *How did I get here?* The round gazebo-like structure enclosed by statues of famous academics sat at the bottom of the campus; it was the place Alice would go to hide away from the world. It gave her comfort to be near something her mother had once touched, though at that moment, terror drowned out any sense of comfort she might have found.

The statue of Madame Curie looming over her sent chills down her spine. Alice pulled her legs to her chest, kicking a bottle of water near her feet.

She picked up the bottle and examined it, thinking about how the cool liquid would soothe her scratchy throat. *Should I drink it?* She examined the cap; the seal hadn't been broken.

She gulped down an unsteady breath. *Someone must have left it, but who? Who would leave me here alone?* Unable to ignore her thirst, Alice took a sip, letting the water coat her throat while calming her frayed nerves.

Alice looked around, trying to remember how she'd gotten here. *The last thing I remember was going to find Kaleb.*

She ran her hands over the ridges of the plastic bottle.

A note.

Kaleb had left me a note.

What did it say?

Her hair fell into her face, and she pushed it out of the way. For the first time, she noticed the dark bruises on her arms. Alice looked closer at them. The bruises were shaped like fingers. Her chest tightened. Her breath caught as the memories rushed toward her.

Kaleb's. It was trashed. The noise in the back of the house. Did I really go inside?

Alice tried to stand, but her legs wobbled under her. She forced herself to walk to a marble bench that sat in the center of the structure before collapsing onto it.

"Did I try to attack Ryan with a shoe?" she asked the bronze statues in front of her.

Einstein, Galileo, and Sir Isaac Newton didn't answer. "What was I thinking?" They looked down at her, judging without saying a word.

"What happened after that?" she asked the statues again.

"You ran."

Alice jumped. *Had the statue talked? No, that's crazy.*

"Who's th-there?"

The voice continued to speak as if she hadn't asked a question. "A side effect of the drug. Turns your trust into fear, or something like that."

Her muscles tightened at the sound of his mirthless laugh.

"I guess you're more of a flight than fight kind of person."

Not ready to deal with the fact that she'd been drugged, Alice concentrated on the now. She reached into her pocket, looking for something she could use as a weapon. The key to Kaleb's car dug into her palm, and Alice gripped it between her fingers, turning her knuckles white, ready for a fight.

A cloud moved across the sky, covering the sun and casting the area into darkness. The shadows morphed the statutes into ghoulish figures, reaching out to grab an unsuspecting victim.

"Come out where I can see you," Alice demanded in a voice that sounded shrill.

The person moved between two statues, stepping off the pedestal onto the brick floor. His feet hit the ground as the sun came out. Its bright rays illuminated the words etched in the structure. Exaltation of Reason. Recognizing the irony of the moment, Alice snorted.

Linc stared at her, searching for something, sanity maybe. Alice wasn't sure. Her heart was racing; she scanned the area for a quick exit. A need—no, an overwhelming urge to run engulfed her. Her mind screamed, *Linc is your friend.* But her body wouldn't listen.

Linc must have seen her panic because he put his hands up, ready to surrender. His voice picked up a southern drawl he rarely used. "Darlin', I'm not here to hurt you." He smiled that charming smile he used to pick up women. "Kaleb sent me."

Alice stood on shaky legs, the key at the ready. Her heart thumped hard against her chest at the mention of Kaleb's name. If Kaleb had sent Linc, did that make him an enemy or a friend? She didn't know. The lines of what was true and what was fear had started to blur. *Maybe I am insane.*

"Why you?"

Linc's Adam's apple bobbed. "To protect you," he sneered.

Alice laughed, not a mirth-filled laugh, but one of those evil-villain-revealing-their-plan-to-take-over-the-world kind of laugh. "Kaleb's the one who shot me up with, whatever."

At least she thought it was Kaleb, but it very well could've been Ryan. Things were too foggy in her mind to know for sure who had done what, but someone had drugged her. That much she was sure of. "Why would I trust anything you say?"

He snorted. "You shouldn't."

That was the last thing she expected to hear, even if it was true.

She let doubt seep into her thoughts. *What do I really know about Linc?* Memories of the past swarmed around her, changing, twisting. *Had he saved me at the lake or had I saved him? No, that was a dream. Wasn't it? It had to be.* She wasn't sure anymore what was real and what wasn't. All she knew was that she needed to run and, if he didn't let her go, to fight.

"There is more going on here than you know." Linc leaned against the edge of the marble pedestal. "You can trust Kaleb. Everything he has done is to protect you."

Alice rolled her eyes. Kaleb wanted her dead. *No, that's the drug talking. Isn't it? Trust to fear, that's what Linc said.* Did that mean she could trust Linc?

"Alice?" Linc snapped his fingers. "Are you still here?"

She nodded. "Mostly."

Linc continued. "Red Queen Inc. is not what you think it is. It's a front for a criminal organization, and Reid Redding is the leader." He sat down cross-legged between Socrates and Aristotle. "The theater and the lake were a test run. I think they're working on a reset for the world. A virus, one that will destroy everything and everyone around them. After a few short months, there will be nothing left but a small group of their choosing ready to rebuild how they see fit."

A sour taste settled in Alice's throat at the thought of anyone being that heartless. She wasn't sure if Linc was telling the truth, but Alice suspected he was. "As the only one to survive WonderLand, trust me, it would take days, not months."

Linc nodded but didn't say anything more. The fear that had been building up inside Alice mixed with the anger that was always boiling below the surface of her calm exterior. It was a sour brew that turned in her stomach.

"Let me get this straight," she said. "Reid Redding, the CEO of the biggest medical research company in the world, is also the leader of a terrorist group. A group that wants to release a deadly virus onto an unsuspecting public, causing horrible, painful deaths."

"Unknowing volunteers," he mumbled.

Alice ignored his statement, not ready to deal with what it meant. "You, Kaleb, and my mother." She hoped she was right about her mother, but it was a guess. One that made sense with what he was saying. She had been the guest of honor, after all, meaning Reid Redding had needed her to be in that theater. "You work for the Task Force."

Linc's eyes shone with surprise at Alice's mention of the Task Force. So, he didn't know that Kaleb had told her about his involvement with them. Alice smiled at Linc, a sense of triumph overriding some of the anger and fear that still plagued her. She didn't agree with Kaleb's views on Reid Redding, not completely; the woman had helped Alice in more ways than she could count. But she had agreed to his stupid green card plan, just in case. *Because he might be right.*

Linc cleared his throat. "Your mother, she wasn't; she didn't know what Reid was doing. Not at first anyway. When she found out, she came to the people I work for, a government-sponsored group you call the Task Force. They specialize in finding people like Reid Redding and destroying them from the inside."

He looked away from Alice, and she noticed how much older Linc looked than her and Kaleb. "The Task Force learned a few weeks after the incident at the theater that Ms. Redding wanted Elizabeth dead. Elizabeth had some evidence against Red Queen, and someone had discovered your mother's involvement with the Task Force." He met her eyes again. "I should have gotten her out sooner."

"What are you talking about?" The warm ball of anger in Alice's belly rose, overriding the fear. For the first time in a long time, she didn't fight it. "The reason my mother is dead," she said through clenched teeth. "It's because she was working for you."

"Not me, the Task Force. My mother was her handler, and by the time she found out that Elizabeth had been compromised, it was too late."

Alice's vision flickered into black and white. Out of habit, she took a deep, calming breath, stopping WonderLand from taking over. *I won't let the virus take control. If I do, I'll never find out what happened.* Alice waited for her lungs to fill with cool air and for the color to take hold of the world around her again before speaking. She wanted to ask who had turned her mother over, but the words wouldn't come out because the anger was still biting her throat. "You and Kaleb are working—"

Linc cleared his throat. "And DeeDee."

"Of course, we can't forget DeeDee. You and Kaleb and DeeDee are working to find the evidence she had so you can...what?"

He smiled at Alice's biting remark before answering her question. "Find a way to bring down the Red Queen and her empire."

Black spots swam in Alice's vision. "Did you really just call her the Red Queen?" She covered her face, telling herself the confusion was because of the ridiculous turn this conversation had taken. But something was wrong. *This isn't the virus.* She knew how to control the virus. This was different, like her body was fighting to stay in one place and her mind in another. "And Tom?" she asked. "Does he know anything about what you're doing?"

"My brother chose a different side when he picked a drug over his family and sent an assassin after me."

Alice winced at Linc's detached tone. *The brothers seemed so close. How could Tom do that? When did Tom do that?*

As if he knew what she'd been thinking, he added, "He has no idea that I know it was him. Just thinks I escaped the Knights grasp and am now under the Task Force protection."

Kaleb's deep voice echoed around them. "And he won't know anything more until we need him to."

That voice, the one that normally gave Alice comfort, slithered across her vertebrae. Alice's heart quickened. No longer able to hold on to reality, her head jerked from one bronze statue to another. The faces of the scientists and philosophers melted away, morphing into the people from the theater.

She bit her cheek, holding on to a scream that knocked at her teeth. Blood filled her mouth, its warm metallic liquid running down her throat, reminding Alice of a dark theater and red streaks flowing from the eyes of her attackers.

She could see the guy with the dark rimmed glasses looming over her, mocking her. Alice's heart drummed a panicked rhythm. *Bats, he was yelling at me about bats.* She covered her ears and rocked. She told herself that he was dead, but the fear crashed in on her, overriding the anger that accompanied those memories.

Alice took a deep breath, trying to calm the cyclone of emotions. The cool outside air trapped inside her lungs turned to lava as the world around her blurred.

Alice ran.

Up the wide sidewalk.

Through the trees.

Colors blurring.
A green blob chasing her.
Kaleb's voice fused with the green. "Damn it."
Reaching out.
Grabbing.
"The Timore. It's still in her system."

Chapter 9

It took all night, but Kaleb found Alice curled up asleep under a big tree that covered most of a small outdoor stage. He knew the benches near the stage were Alice's favorite places to study and one of the few places she was at peace, the rotunda with the creepy statues being the other. It should have been the first place he looked. He picked her up, grateful she didn't wake up but cuddled in closer.

"What am I going to do?" he asked himself.

Alice mumbled something in her sleep, wrapping her arms around his neck.

He walked across the empty campus, grateful for the early hour and few people to question him. As he walked, the sunrays started to peek up from behind the mountains, lighting his way. He looked up at her apartment. Alice needed to disappear, and he was going with her. The Task Force would have to bring Redding to justice without him.

The Timore makeup was similar to WonderLand, and since Alice was immune, it shouldn't have worked. That was why Ryan had used it on her. To give them time. To get her away from Tom's prying eyes. The plan was for Ryan to inject Alice while Kaleb told her how to act. When Tom's guard was down, he would tell Alice to run.

Well, she ran, but it was out of fear and without direction. She was lucky; other than a few cuts and scrapes, Alice seemed fine.

Tom. Kaleb shook his head. He still couldn't believe it. Tom had sold Linc out for one of Dr. Turtle's designer drugs. But for whatever reason, Tom hadn't told any of Joseph's goons about Kaleb's or Ryan's involvement with the Task Force, and, for now, both their covers remained intact.

Kaleb pulled his car keys from his front pocket; Alice had dropped them when she ran from him the night before. He tried to open the passenger door and not wake Alice, but it proved to be more difficult than he thought. Somehow, he managed to get the door open and her in the passenger seat without smacking either of their heads on the door frame.

Sitting in the driver's seat, he thought, *Now what?*

Tom knew the Timore worked on Alice. Dr. Turtle and Ms. Redding would have been told by now. Kaleb wouldn't be able to shield her like he did at the lake. They would bring her in at any cost, and that scared him. Kaleb looked over at Alice's sleeping form. That drug shouldn't have worked, not if Alice was immune to the virus. *What did it mean?* He couldn't leave Alice alone, not now.

How am I going to do this? Hide her from the world?

Kaleb's phone pinged with an incoming message. He was almost afraid to look at it. He'd sent Linc and DeeDee to search for Alice. He pulled out his phone, hoping it was one of them checking in and not his father. Joseph hadn't called him yet, not since they'd lost Alice the first time, but Kaleb knew it was coming. Thankfully, it was Marci.

Supplies in the back seat. Good Luck!

Kaleb looked behind him. Sure enough, there was a case of water, a box of food, his backpack, and a new laptop in the back seat.

Alice's duffel bag and cell phone were also in the back. He tried to figure out how she had gotten into his locked car and how she knew what he would do or that he would go with Alice. Then he remembered it was Marci.

His phone pinged again.

PS- Didn't have time with the phone. Get rid of it soon.

He would stop at the strip mall and buy some disposable phones before they left town. Better to get new phones here before anyone suspected they had run.

The phone pinged again.

PPS- I let DeeDee know.

Kaleb put the key in the ignition, the white rabbit foot dangling above his thigh, and started the car. *One less thing to worry about.*

A short time later, he pulled into a parking space in front of the little local grocery store. The store had a small electronics section where he could buy a new phone and withdraw some cash from an ATM inside.

He looked over at Alice, wondering if he should wake her. Alice stirred next to him but didn't wake. Kaleb didn't want to leave her alone, but they needed to get out of town quickly. He reached behind him, pulling a plastic water bottle and a protein bar from the back seat. With a black sharpie from his backpack he wrote the words "drink me" on the bottle and "eat me" on the protein bar.

In case she wakes up, he told himself.

He got out of the car and walked into the cool air-conditioned store. A lone cashier smiled an it's-too-early-to-be-this-nice smile at him. "Is there something I can help you find?" she asked.

He shook his head and moved toward the electronics section. There wasn't much of a selection: a couple of flip phones, batteries, and a pair of headphones. He grabbed one of the phones, a basic black one that displayed the time in a little window on the front. *Back to basics. I guess it will have to work.*

Kaleb thought about what his life had become. To put it simply, it was a disaster, one that led him to trust few and lie to the woman he loved. *Not that she has any idea how I feel about her.* Now he was going to bring her into the world he had tried so hard to keep her from. Being on the run was going to be hard, but Kaleb hoped it would be a new beginning for them. He could tell her about his involvement with Red Queen Inc. and all the horrible things he had done, including the day her mother had died. In time, he hoped, Alice would understand that he didn't know what was going to happen.

Kaleb paid for his few items and walked out of the store with a new sense of...what? It wasn't hope. Maybe possibility. Whatever it was, for the first time, he felt something besides the constant fear and anger that underlined every part of his life.

He looked over at the black car that had once belonged to his mother and smiled. This was going to work. There was no other way and no one to talk him out of it this time.

The guttural purr of a black motorcycle pulling into the space next to Dorothy pulled Kaleb back to the real world. He knew before the black helmet was removed that it was Ryan. What he didn't know was why he was here, at this store, at this hour. It didn't make sense. He should be in class, at some RA meeting, or even in bed. Not here. Not now.

Ryan pulled off his helmet. "I thought you left."

"On my way out now."

A smile moved across Ryan's lips, one that didn't quite meet his eyes and made Kaleb's stomach turn. He looked around the parking lot, still empty. Not unusual for this time of day. Something was off about Ryan.

"Did you get Alice?" Ryan asked.

Kaleb thought about Alice asleep in the car behind Ryan. *How had he not seen her?*

There was something about Ryan's eyes that didn't seem right. Kaleb considered telling Ryan the truth, or that he hadn't found her yet but was sure she was still in town. It was better if Ryan didn't know that Kaleb knew where Alice was.

"No, and I'm not sure where to find her."

Ryan motioned to the bag in Kaleb's hand.

"Picking up a few things before getting out of town. You know, before Tom blows my cover too."

"Too bad." Ryan snorted.

Kaleb stared at Ryan, waiting for him to explain.

"Reid sent out the Knights to bring her in. Their orders are dead or alive."

Black spots overtook Kaleb's vision. The Knights. Why would she send the Knights? Yes, they would bring Alice in, but it wouldn't be alive or even in one piece.

They took pleasure in causing pain in the name of science. Kaleb should know; he'd seen them at work. It was why his mother wasn't around anymore.

The memory of the last time he saw her crashed to the surface.

Light peeked through the slats of the closet door, her lingering perfume wrapping around him, comforting him. Shattered dishes and broken glass crunched under booted feet outside the closet door. Sticky red on Kaleb's hand, blood... So much blood... And the screaming...

Ryan's voice broke through Kaleb's memories. "If one of us were the one to bring her in, we could guarantee she stays alive." Ryan looked toward Kaleb's car, and Kaleb's pulse jumped. "Too bad you don't know how to find her."

"Yeah, too bad."

If Alice was going to survive, Kaleb had to take her to the only person who knew how to hide from the Knights. It wasn't going to be easy, but it was the only way he knew how to protect Alice. But first, he needed to find a way to get rid of Ryan.

Ryan took a step toward Kaleb; a silver tube in his right hand caught the light, the word *Thavasi* printed in bold font on it. It was one of Dr. Turtle's designer drugs that screwed with your emotions. Kaleb tried to remember which emotion the drug was supposed to manipulate. The fact that it was in a tube meant it was a cream.

"What are you doing?" Kaleb asked.

Ryan shook his head as if to clear his mind.

Had he gotten it on his skin?

Ryan grunted. "The Task Force, they're bringing me in. The Knights change things, and they feel like it's no longer safe for me at Red Queen."

"Why here?" Kaleb motioned to the stores, hoping to distract Ryan from the car and Alice.

"To keep my cover. If they capture me, then I can go back in." Ryan glared at Kaleb. "Are you that stupid?"

Ryan's words sparked Kaleb's memory about the Thavasi and what it was supposed to do, changing admiration to disgust. Considering the way he was acting, Ryan had gotten some on his skin. Kaleb would worry about that later; for now, he could use that disgust that Ryan felt to his advantage.

Using his most condescending voice, Kaleb said, "Maybe you should go inside and set up or whatever you were going to do."

Ryan clenched his fist, a fight brewing in his eyes. He released a deep breath before tearing his gaze from Kaleb's and stomping off toward the store, mumbling something about how that was what he was doing.

Kaleb climbed into the car and grabbed his phone to send a quick message to Marci, warning her that Ryan had been dosed with Thavasi. Marci would pass the information on to the Task Force for him.

The phone vibrated in his hand moments after he sent the message. Kaleb thought it would be Marci scolding him for not getting rid of the phone already. It wasn't.

Joseph's sun-worn face glared up at him. Kaleb's finger hovered over the ignore option. *If he thinks I'm still out looking for Alice, it might buy us some time.*

Against his better judgment, Kaleb answered the phone. "What?"

"Where are you?" he barked.

"Around."

"Kaleb, could we please get through one conversation without hostility?"

There was something in Joseph's voice that made Kaleb stop and think. The tone reminded Kaleb of the dad he had before Red Queen Inc., when his mom and brothers were still around, when they were happy. "Fine."

"Good. Look, I need you to come in. If you've found Alice, bring her in with you."

He looked over at Alice's sleeping form. *So, the old man didn't want to make peace. He wanted Alice.* "She's gone. And before you ask, I have no idea where she went."

"I'm sorry, son. I know you care for her."

I bet he's sorry Alice is gone, but not for my sake. "Why do you need me to come in?"

"If you come in, I might be able to convince Reid to call off the Knights. She sent them to collect you and Alice."

Kaleb gripped the steering wheel, cursing himself for answering the phone. If he didn't do what his father asked, Joseph would know Kaleb was lying about Alice. There would be no way of hiding her then. Joseph knew all of Kaleb's hiding spots. He would have to go in. It would buy Alice time to get out, time to find his mother. It was the only way Kaleb could keep her safe.

Kaleb looked at Alice, her dark hair covering her face. He would find her again.

"Call the Knights off. I'm coming in."

"You have fifteen minutes to get here or no deal." Joseph hung up before Kaleb could respond, getting the last word in, like always.

"Jerk," Kaleb called out to the dead air before sending an encrypted message to his brother Markus, begging him to help. *He'll know how to get Alice to where she needs to go.*

Alice was still sound asleep in the seat next to him. He tried to wake her to explain, but he knew that fear—the emotion the Timore brought on—had exhausted her. She wouldn't wake up until her body recovered. He needed a way to make sure Alice met up with Markus. If he set Markus's coordinates as an alarm on Alice's phone, she would see it. Kaleb reached behind the seat and grabbed Alice's phone.

Someone banged on the window, causing Kaleb to jump and knock the bag over. Its contents covered Alice's phone. He turned to find Ryan peering into the passenger window, pointing at Alice's sleeping form. *Damn it.*

Kaleb looked at the keys in the ignition and thought about driving away, but he knew it wouldn't work. He'd already wasted more time than he should, and Ryan would follow, giving Kaleb no choice but to bring Alice in.

He opened the driver's-side door and walked around the car to the passenger side, where Ryan stood. Before Ryan could say a word, Kaleb punched him in the face. He'd hoped to catch him off guard enough to get an advantage. Ryan was a good fighter and had kicked Kaleb's butt a number of times while sparring. But luck or the drugs were on Kaleb's side. Ryan didn't fight but slid down the side of the car, his eyes rolled back. *Out cold.*

Kaleb dragged Ryan's unconscious body to the side of the building, checking his pockets for his keys to the motorcycle. "Sorry, can't have you helping Red Queen get to Alice."

Kaleb got back into the car and looked at the clock on the dash; he was running out of time. He tried to find Alice's phone while the ticking of time rang in his ears.

He couldn't find it.

The green card he left Alice yesterday had tumbled out with the stack of clothes. Kaleb looked down at his watch. Eight minutes. That was all he had left. The card would have to do.

He scribbled the longitude and latitude of the place Alice would meet Markus and placed it next to the protein bar he had left for her earlier. *She'll go this time,* he reassured himself.

Kaleb pulled on Ryan's black helmet and climbed onto his motorcycle. The engine roared to life underneath him.

He looked back one last time at what could have been before speeding off toward the disaster he called life.

CHAPTER 10

Alice opened her eyes expecting to see a tree-lined forest, not the local grocery store, through the glass windshield of Kaleb's car. Its metal shell protected her from the rain-soaked world outside, and a pine-scented air freshener hanging from the rearview mirror fooled her sleep-deprived mind. Alice pulled down the visor and looked at herself in the mirror. Sticks and dirt littered her hair, and her face was stained with dirt and tears. *What happened?*

The alarm on her phone sang out a muffled tune. Alice patted her pockets, but it wasn't there. The song started again, and Alice listened, trying to narrow down where the noise was coming from. The music came from somewhere within the green duffel bag she'd packed the day before, which lay open on the floor of the back seat. She reached into the bag, knocking over something in the cupholder as she fumbled around for the phone.

Alice slid her finger across the purple screen to silence the alarm.

The last thing I remember was Linc and Kaleb, something. She pinched the bridge of her nose. A dull thump danced behind her eyes, and her mouth tasted of old pennies. Looking around the always clean car for clues, Alice tried to remember how she'd gotten there.

She knew something terrible had happened and that Kaleb was somehow involved. What it was, was still a blur. An image of a green card popped into her mind. Kaleb had left it for her, but what did it say? Her hand brushed across the rectangular package of a protein bar she knocked out of the cupholder earlier, and her stomach growled. *When was the last time I ate?*

Alice grabbed the bar; "eat me" had been written with a black sharpie in Kaleb's curvy handwriting across the tan wrapper of her favorite flavor.

She bit into the thick cake-like bar wrapped in a thin layer of creamy white chocolate. It tasted like ambrosia to her empty stomach. Alice chewed the bar, letting the chocolate melt in her mouth. As she ate, the rain changed from a downpour to a slight drizzle. Alice's throat was dry, and she reached for the water bottle in a nearby cupholder. She clasped the bottle in her warm hands, reading the words written on the side. "Drink me." Alice chuckled to herself as she took the lid off, the clicking of the breaking seal the only other noise in the car. She took a sip of the water and looked out the window, wondering what to do now.

The green card plan had been put into play, but she couldn't remember why. Other than the bag in the back seat, a bag she remembered packing, there were no clues on what to do next.

A woman with long blonde hair in a high ponytail walking into the store caught Alice's attention. *DeeDee? Hadn't Linc said she had something to do with all of this?* That sounded right. *Should I follow her? She might know where Kaleb is.*

She looked over at the driver's seat, Kaleb's keys hanging from the ignition. *Or do I take the car and run like Kaleb told me to yesterday?*

Alice pocketed the keys. *Maybe DeeDee knows where Kaleb is.* She opened the door, letting the smell of wet concrete mixed with rain wash away the artificial pine smell of Kaleb's car.

Goosebumps moved down her arms when she stepped into the cool air-conditioned store, but not because of the cold. The store was empty. It wasn't unusual for a Saturday morning—Alice's favorite time to shop—but even Madge the cashier was missing.

Unsure where to look for DeeDee, Alice went right toward the produce section. It was easy to scan and empty, not a soul in sight.

Next was the snack aisle. The floor was covered with stacked boxes ready to be unloaded. A few of them lay open as if someone had started to stock the shelves and abandoned it midway through. Alice kept going, passing three aisles in the same condition.

She stood at the end of the canned food aisle, the emptiness of the store getting to her. *This was a bad idea; I should go back to the car.* Turning toward the front of the store, Alice heard DeeDee's singsong voice. It sounded like she was on the phone.

Alice listened to the one-sided conversation.

"You're late."

"I'm in aisle ten."

"Make it quick."

Turning the corner to aisle ten, Alice found DeeDee standing alone in the center of the cereal aisle. Her cold, unforgiving eyes appraised Alice. "What?" Alice asked. DeeDee took a step toward her, and Alice took a step back. The look in DeeDee's eyes—it was different, not her normal sad watchful gaze.

"Alice?" She raised her hands as if to surrender. Then she glanced behind Alice before speaking with a shaky voice. "What are you doing here?"

"I, ah..." Alice didn't know what to say. Now that she had found DeeDee, she wasn't sure why she had followed her. Answers, maybe? If Linc had been telling the truth, DeeDee had been a part of everything horrible that had happened to Alice in the last four years. *He also said she was trying to help.* "I have no idea what's going on. I woke up in Kaleb's car. I'm missing hours of my life, and then I saw you," Alice rambled. "I had hoped you would... I don't know."

DeeDee bit her lip. "You need to leave, Alice, go far, far away from here."

"But..."

She heard DeeDee mutter, "I'm going to kill Rabbit." She looked behind her. "Look, Alice, I can't talk right now. Do you remember the first week I was here and those pledges got involved in that prank war and how I was ditched at that gas station in the middle of nowhere?"

Alice nodded.

"Meet me there in two hours."

"But—"

DeeDee pushed Alice in the direction of the exit. "Alice, please go."

Alice walked down the aisle, wondering, not for the first time, what was going on and why everyone was trying to get rid of her. *Why won't they just tell me what's happening?*

A slimy hand clasped her wrist. Alice screamed, pulling her arms from the person's grasp, falling on her butt in the process.

Ryan's tall form loomed over her, his eyes shining with hatred. His hands, covered with purple surgical gloves and blue goo, reached for her. Sliding across the cold linoleum floor, she tried to forget about Ryan's grip and the burning sensation that whirled across her skin.

What was on his hand, and why did it hurt so much?

Light footsteps sounded behind Alice, bringing with them the flowery scent that followed DeeDee everywhere she went. Warm fingers wrapped around Alice's shoulders, helping her to her feet. Alice stared at Ryan, trying to ignore the burning on her arm, not wanting to give him the satisfaction of knowing he'd affected her.

"What happened to your face?" DeeDee asked Ryan.

He grumbled something about Kaleb and touched the dark bluish-purple bruise forming on his cheek.

DeeDee looked down at Alice's arm. The slimy substance on Ryan's hands still shimmered under the fluorescent lights. "You brought the Thavasi."

Ryan looked Alice up and down, making her skin crawl. This thing—he couldn't be a person—had licked her. Seeing him now, Alice knew he'd drugged her. He had put something on her skin that felt like she'd been branded with a hot poker. Alice swallowed back her disgust, squared her shoulders, and opened her mouth to say something venomous. No, that didn't feel right. Neither did the nice-ish things that scraped off the surface of her mind. *Something's wrong.*

DeeDee moved to stand next to Alice, close enough for her to smell DeeDee's flowery perfume. For the first time, the scent made her stomach roll. *This doesn't make sense. I have the same perfume. It's not my favorite, but it's never made me sick.*

DeeDee's whispered voice stirred the hair on her neck. "Don't trust anything you feel from this moment on."

"What? Why?"

"Your arm." She motioned to Alice.

Alice looked down at where Ryan had grabbed her. The blue substance that had been on Ryan's gloves was disappearing, absorbing into her skin, leaving behind the light pink color of a fresh sunburn. The skin even held the heat of a fresh sunburn, dancing its way up her arm and through her body.

"DeeDee." Ryan tsked. "My dear duchess, I expected this from Rabbit. But you?" He glared at DeeDee. "You, I thought, had more loyalty than this, to turn on your sister, your family, and for what?" He took a step toward Alice, and she cringed. "This girl."

"It was your job to bring her in, not mine." DeeDee waved to Alice with indifference. "It's not my fault you couldn't bring this little pineapple in."

Pineapple? Did DeeDee just call me a pineapple?

Alice stared at Ryan, curious if he would say anything about it.

He stared at her, and his lips moved into a wide smile, sending a shiver down Alice's spine.

Alice's heart quickened, and heat rose to her cheeks.

Touching her face, hiding the blush, Alice studied Ryan. Freckles covered his nose and cheeks. His eyes were a dark brown, and they had little specks of amber and green. But it was his smile that made her heart jump and body tingle. It brightened the room, with his perfect white teeth and the slight dimple on the right side of his face. If not for a dark bruise forming along his jaw, he would be perfect.

Outrage bubbled in her gut that someone had messed up her Ryan's perfect face.

Wait... What? His what? I... No, I can't be thinking about Ryan's dimples. Ryan, the non-person, who licked me, and drugged me! This has to be what DeeDee meant when she said not to trust my emotions. It's the only explanation.

Ryan demanded, "Give me the girl, and I'll be on my way."

Alice almost stepped toward him before reminding herself once again not to trust her emotions.

DeeDee ignored his demand. "While we're on the subject of Alice, what is it that makes her so special?" she asked. "So what, WonderLand didn't work on her. She's immune. Big deal. I don't get it."

I'm not, but Dr. Turtle is the only person who knows I still have the virus.

Ryan's voice wavered. "It's not important."

"So, it's true, then; you're nothing more than my sister's lackey." DeeDee examined her nails as if she were bored. "And here I thought you had real power in the organization, not just a part in her deck of cards."

He moved closer, fists clenched at his sides. "I'm not a lackey."

She shrugged. "If you say so."

Alice watched Ryan's jaw tick, and he gave Deedee a cold, calculating look. She'd gone too far.

Ryan lunged forward, knocking boxes of cereal to the floor.

DeeDee pushed Alice behind her moments before Ryan slammed into the aisle next to them.

Brightly colored puffed sugary cereal skated across the scuffed tile.

Ryan stood up, ready to go after DeeDee again.

The aisle filled with men dressed in black military-like armor, guns pointed at Ryan, red dots painted across his chest.

Alice's heart quickened. In her head, she pled with Ryan not to move. *Don't move, just stay down.*

The men moved closer, fruit-shaped puffs crunching under their boots. Trapped Ryan turned in circles, a look of disgust plastered on his face, but all Alice could think was how adorable he was even when he had lost.

DeeDee motioned to the men around her. "Ryan, the way I see it, you have two choices. Come in peacefully, or one of these men would be happy to loan you a bullet."

Linc's soft, muffled voice came from behind the mask closest to Alice. "My vote would be the bullet."

But he's your friend.

Ryan looked around the aisle, panic on his face, as he reached into his jacket. A shot rang through the air, and Alice screamed and lunged toward him.

Linc pushed her to the ground, his warm arms forcing her to stay down. She fought her captor, clawing at the floor. Cereal crunched under her palms, and the cold linoleum under her fingers cooled her warm skin. She needed to get to Ryan!

Alice shook her head, clearing her mind for a moment. *What am I doing?* Linc's strong arms wrapped around her waist, dragging Alice away. He dropped her into a plastic folding chair.

Alice took two shaky breaths. "Is he...dead?"

Linc snorted. "No."

He knelt down in front of Alice and flashed a bright light into her eyes. "Drink," he demanded, handing her a bottle of water.

"Is she okay?" DeeDee asked Linc before leaning over Alice.

She smelled of Froot Loops and summer; drops of red speckled her white shirt. Alice thought it might be blood, and she hoped it was DeeDee's, not Ryan's.

Linc stood and motioned to Alice. "What happened? Where's Kaleb? He was supposed to disappear with her."

"Me? Disappear with Kaleb? Yuck." Her stomach rolled at the idea of Kaleb. "Why would I want to be anywhere near him?"

DeeDee and Linc ignored Alice, and she was fine with that; they weren't important.

Linc looked at Alice. "Marci said Kaleb and Alice were headed out of town and were disappearing for a while. I thought since she's here, maybe he is too."

DeeDee knelt down in front of Alice.

Alice was humming some pop love song that she didn't know the words to, but it reminded her of Ryan. That's all that mattered.

"Where's Kaleb?"

Alice looked at DeeDee, confused by the question. "I don't want to talk about Kaleb." He was nothing more to her than a fly that buzzed around her, making a pest of himself. Alice wanted to know about Ryan, where he was, what he was thinking, which soap he used, and what his favorite color was. "Where's Ryan?" she squalled.

No one answered her, of course. They all treated her like she was a child. *Fine, I won't talk. Maybe if I'm quiet, they'll say where Ryan is, and then I can rescue him. Oh my gosh, that would be so romantic.*

Someone jogged up to Linc and handed him a silver tube of what looked like toothpaste. It was the same tube Ryan had in his hand when they shot him. Reading the words on the bottle out loud, he shook his head. "Thavasi, damn."

DeeDee took the tube from Linc. "This is the stuff that was on Alice's arm. What does it do?"

Linc didn't answer.

So, of course, DeeDee started to ramble. Alice hated that about her; silence was not DeeDee's thing.

"Linc, do you know what it does?" DeeDee asked. "No one ever told me. No one ever tells me anything. I mean, I know the drugs coming out of Red Queen right now affect emotions." DeeDee looked at Alice and then back to Linc, who didn't seem to be listening. "That's why I told her not to trust her own emotions. But I have no idea what any of them do. Linc?"

Linc paced back and forth, his heavy boots clomping down on the tile reminding Alice of a prancing horse. "I can't figure it out. Why drug Alice? What is Reid trying to do?"

DeeDee asked again, "Linc, what emotion?"

He looked down at Alice. She could feel a goofy smile on her face, but she didn't care. She couldn't stop thinking about her future with Ryan. They'd have a beach wedding, of course. A house in the suburbs and a couple of kids. When the kids were older, they'd see the world together.

"It's like all the other drugs, turning one emotion into a different one, but in this case, it's disgust into admiration." He sighed. "She can't help us. She won't help us. Not with Kaleb anyway. Not until the drug is out of her system."

"What do we do then?"

"The only thing we can do is wait."

CHAPTER
11

Kaleb looked around the security office of Red Queen Inc. His father stood in the corner, arms folded, glaring. Kaleb had nothing to say. Joseph assured him the Knights had been called off. Kaleb wouldn't believe it, not until he heard from Markus that Alice was safe.

Joseph had one of his goons handcuff Kaleb to a chair, a black rolling chair of all things. He moved his arm and tugged on his restraint, inwardly rolling his eyes. *This is ridiculous.* He wasn't sure why they would cuff him to a rolling chair.

Unable to deal with the anger radiating from his father any longer and wanting to annoy Joseph at the same time, Kaleb spun the chair in circles. The gray walls, bookshelf, and security monitors blended into long squiggly lines.

The chair stopped. Gryff, the bulking thug who headed the Knights, used his beefy arms to hold the back of the chair as he glared down at Kaleb.

"Enough," Joseph growled.

Kaleb planted his feet firmly on the ground and grinned at his father. He'd gotten to the old man. It wasn't much of a win, but it was enough for now.

He watched the computer screens, the images changing every few seconds. A lab tech grabbed a vial from the glass freezer.

Madison clocked in for the day. Dr. Turtle helped a dark-haired girl onto an examination table.

"You didn't think we would let you leave," Joseph's voice boomed. "Not with everything you've seen."

Kaleb met his father's smug gaze and shrugged. *Of course not, but I had to try. It was my only way to save Alice.*

"Come on, boy. You're smarter than this." Joseph ran his fingers through his thinning hair. "All the evidence you've collected over the years and still no arrests. I know you gave it to your little Task Force, and nothing happened. Haven't you ever wondered why?"

Looks like Tom told Joseph about my involvement in the Task Force. Great. Forgetting for a moment about the restraints, Kaleb tried to fold his arms. He shouldn't be surprised Joseph knew about the Task Force. Tom had turned in his own brother; of course he'd tell them about the Task Force. *Good thing the only people Tom knew were on both sides were Linc, Ryan, and me.*

Pinching the bridge of his nose, Gryff glared at Kaleb. "The Task Force is nothing more than a way to deal with the disenchanted members of Red Queen Inc., like you and your friend Linc. It's a sham organization that actually takes orders from us."

Kaleb chuckled. *This is rich, using the same tactics Joseph drilled in me about interrogation.* "You already know everything, so I might as well tell you what I know. Right?"

Kaleb stood up to leave, forgetting for a moment he was cuffed to the chair and dragging the rolling chair behind him.

"Like you said, Joseph, I'm smarter than that. I know all your tricks." Looking back at the chair, he thought, *Even if I don't look like it at the moment.*

Joseph blocked his path, his phone held out in front of Kaleb, the text message icon lighting up the screen. "Look for yourself."

He didn't want to look at the phone. Kaleb knew his father; whatever was on the screen would change things. Even if they weren't true, a seed of doubt would be planted. *I'll just look at the phone number*, he told himself. *If it's not one I know, then I won't look at the message.*

DeeDee's phone number lit up the screen. *It could be nothing*, he told himself as he sat back down in the chair he was attached to.

Kaleb took the phone from Joseph and scanned the last three messages, all sent in the last hour. Not wanting to believe his father, Kaleb looked at the messages twice, looking for any indication they were fake.

Alice found.

Thavasi Test successful.

Package on its way.

Kaleb ran his hand through his hair.

This couldn't be true. DeeDee helped me. She wouldn't do this, not to Alice. Not after what we saw in the theater. It has to be a trick. Joseph had someone hack her phone or something.

But then again, DeeDee wasn't supposed to have been at the lake. She had called Kaleb the morning of and begged him to take her.

Kaleb looked at his father's cold eyes and knew Joseph had been aware of Kaleb's involvement with the Task Force all along. *Was it his idea to use Alice to bring me back in?*

The anger Kaleb had kept in check for the last few years surfaced, ready to boil over. *It's fine. So what if DeeDee knows Alice has been found? I never trusted the Task Force*, he reminded himself. *Not completely. That's why I brought Marci on. That's why I didn't give them the flash drive I stole from Dr. Turtle. It was my insurance, in case something happened to me.*

Kaleb played DeeDee's text messages over in his head. He needed something to use against his father, to gain back some ground; he couldn't let Joseph win. Alice needed his help.

He replayed the conversation he had had with Ryan in the parking lot. Nothing jumped out at him as important, but he'd had a tube. *What was it?* Kaleb remembered seeing the screw-on white cap, the silver package shining in the sunlight. Bold letters—THAVASI.

He swallowed the bitter taste of bile that had come up,

remembering the one and only time he'd been exposed to Thavasi. It had been awful fawning over... He couldn't even complete the thought, it was that bad.

DeeDee's text had said **Thavasi Test successful.** It took all his willpower to hide the rage bubbling inside him. He didn't want to believe they would test another drug on Alice, especially after what happened with the Timore, but he knew it was true. Kaleb buried his emotions and met his father's eyes with a smile plastered on his face.

"Interesting, the Thavasi worked on Alice. I thought she would've been immune," Kaleb said with a tone of indifference. "Guess Ryan turned into a useful asset testing two drugs on Alice in less than twenty-four hours."

Joseph looked Kaleb up and down as if he were trying to decide something.

Package on its way. *Who or what was the Package? Where was it?* He wasn't sure, but he had a horrible feeling the package was Alice.

His father bent over, and Kaleb held back a flinch, remembering the sting of Joseph's fist on his face. Joseph had only hit Kaleb that one time after the incident at the theater, but Kaleb had been unsure of his father ever since.

The handcuffs that had been attached to him and the chair fell to the floor. Gryff's deep laugh bounced off the cement walls. Kaleb glared at the hulking men. He stood up and rubbed his wrist as he tried to figure out what he was laughing about.

Gryff turned and stared at one of the security monitors, his back to Kaleb and Joseph as he spoke. "Ryan's done more in two days than that idiot Turtle ever did." He turned to face them. "Too bad we're going to have to kill him." Gryff huffed.

"Why would you kill Ryan?" Kaleb asked.

Before Gryff could answer, the door to the security office slammed open, causing everyone but Gryff to jump.

Dr. Turtle stumbled into the room. His face was red and swollen from exertion. His green button-up shirt was covered in sweat, and the matching tie hung loosely around his neck. He fell into the black rolling chair Kaleb had been cuffed to moments before. Words rushed out of him between wheezed breaths.

Kaleb was only able to understand two stuttered words. "Released... WonderLand..."

They all looked up at the wall of security monitors. A lone screen in the far left corner showed thick pink smoke rolling down a white and gray hall. It slithered onto the next screen, clasping it wispy tentacles around its victims. A blonde lab tech looked up at the camera, her blue eyes shining with fear, begging for help she knew would never come. A silent scream left her lipstick-stained lips moments before the smoke consumed her.

Kaleb clasped the desk in front of him, unable to look away, while the smoke covered its next victim. He knew he should do something, but there was a protocol. A reason Turtle had come here. Like the theater, Kaleb was stuck. Only this time there was no DeeDee to turn off the screen.

A sound of metal scraping metal behind him yanked Kaleb out of the sticky puddle of his emotions. He turned toward the noise. Gryff and his father had black hazmat suits in their hands. Joseph pulled the dark suit up his legs and met Kaleb's eyes. "I have to get to Reid."

"No," Kaleb argued. "You can't."

His father may not have been the best man or even one Kaleb liked, but he was still his dad, and he didn't want him to die. Not like that. No one deserved to die that way, under the madness of WonderLand. Kaleb looked back at the screen, the pink smoke claiming another victim.

Joseph zipped up his suit. "I'll be fine."

Kaleb stared down at the floor, images of the theater flashing in his head, the babbling of the Infected, followed by violence and a lot of death. No survivors, except Alice. Either you succumbed to the virus, or the Infected found you.

Joseph placed a roll of duct tape in Kaleb's hand. "For the door," he said.

He turned to face Turtle and in a commanding voice said, "The second we step out that door you press the red button." Meeting Kaleb's eyes, he said, "That's an order."

Kaleb nodded. He knew he'd press the button, locking all the doors in the building, leaving Joseph to wander the halls with the Infected. It was signing his father's death warrant and saving as many people in the building by trapping them in the rooms they occupied.

Kaleb watched as Joseph pulled on the dark mask that would protect him from the gas but not the Infected and walked out the door, Gryff following close behind.

CHAPTER 12

Alice sat at a long metal table; a large mirror covered the wall in front of her. Her hand hovered over an open notebook, the page covered in swirly letters and hearts. Many of the hearts had Ryan+Alice in the center. *It's my handwriting!* She flipped through the pages. *This has to be some kind of joke. Twenty pages,* she counted, *filled with lies.* On what planet would she ever feel anything but disgust toward Ryan? She pushed the notebook off the table. It hit the concrete floor.

She looked around the room trying to remember not only what had happened but how she'd gotten here. Feeling like she was being watched, Alice looked at the large mirror in front of her, her eyes shimmering—what she thought was a side effect of WonderLand—in the glossy surface. The door behind Alice opened with a squeak. She watched Linc's reflection as he walked through the door. She was surprised to see him dressed in black from head to toe instead of the bright colors he favored.

Linc sat down with a huff in the chair across from Alice but didn't say anything. His dark hair was tousled around his head as if he had been running his hands through it. His eyebrows rose, and a smile lit his face when he saw the crumpled notebook on the floor. "Is it safe to say you are no longer mooning over Ryan?"

Alice met Linc's eyes. "What the hell was that about?"

"Thavasi." DeeDee slipped into the room. "It's one of the drugs from the lab in Red Queen Inc. A failed attempt to treat the victims of the WonderLand." She sat in the chair next to Linc and placed a blue file on the table.

"WonderLand? As in the virus that was released in the theater? The one that was supposed to be destroyed," Alice said.

DeeDee exchanged a look with Linc before nodding.

So Reid lied to me about the virus being destroyed, and the Task Force knew it. Alice swallowed her frustration. "Timore—the drug Linc told me about, the one Ryan injected into me—is that also a failed attempt?" she asked.

Linc straightened. "You remember our conversation. That's good. I was worried the fear might have overwhelmed you, causing a loss of memory."

DeeDee didn't answer Alice's question. "We don't know much about the drugs and viruses coming out of Red Queen," she said. "Just a few things that people inside Red Queen were willing to share." She opened the file. "Timore: trust to fear. Thavasi: disgust into admiration, or vice versa."

Linc chuckled. "But in your case, it was more like puppy love."

DeeDee looked down at the notebook on the floor and smirked. "Ryan made quite an impression on you. Do you mind if I ask what he did?"

"To start, he licked me." Alice looked down at her arm; faint red lines marked her skin. "Then drugged me. Twice."

Linc sat forward. "Alice, why didn't you run when Kaleb told you to?"

Alice shrugged.

Why hadn't I run? It was a good question. She had started to pack. The bag was even in the back seat of Kaleb's car, though she wasn't sure how the bag had gotten there. Alice thought about why she hadn't left, but everything that had happened over the last twenty-four hours was foggy. A side effect of the drugs, maybe. She wasn't sure. The only thing she could think of was it didn't make sense to leave without a good plan, and the green card plan wasn't a good plan.

There had to be more to it.

I wanted answers, not a command. Red Queen poked and prodded me for years. Dr. Turtle was encouraging me to pretend I didn't have the virus. Then there was the whole letting-Kaleb-take-the risk-to-get-answers-for-me thing. Seeing that guy stumble out of the woods infected with something that Reid had told me was destroyed and Kaleb telling me to leave without an explanation, I realized the only way I would get answers was to get them myself.

Of course, Alice didn't say any of this out loud.

She watched DeeDee, who kept adjusting her shirt, pulling at the buttons.

Alice didn't trust her. DeeDee was holding something back, something important. And Linc. Well, Alice still wasn't sure how much she should or could tell him. He'd been there when Alice woke up after the Timore thing, and she hadn't run. That meant on some level, Alice didn't trust him.

She asked the question that had been in the back of her mind since finding that awful notebook full of doodles in her handwriting. "Where's Kaleb?"

The last time Alice remembered seeing Kaleb was when Linc was telling her about the Timore, surrounded by bronze statues and an overwhelming need to flee. The sight of Kaleb, the only person she trusted completely, woke up some primal fear that caused her to run as fast and as hard as she could.

DeeDee's chair scraped the floor as she stood. "No one has seen or heard from Rabbit since..."

Linc exchanged a look with DeeDee. "Alice, after you ran from me, Kaleb sent Marci a message. He told her he'd found you in the library and was taking you to a safe place."

Alice remembered waking up in Kaleb's car earlier that day. She had sticks in her hair and dirt on her face. *If Kaleb had found me in the library, why were there sticks in my hair? If I was in a public place, wouldn't someone have called the police at my crazed behavior? Kaleb couldn't have found me at the library. Why would he lie to Marci?*

DeeDee sat back down. "Marci left me a message letting me know Kaleb was leaving with you and not coming back." She opened and closed the folder on the table in front of her. "I thought that was the end. Then you showed up at the grocery store, and Kaleb is nowhere to be found." DeeDee pushed the file across the table to Alice.

Alice ran her fingers across the edge of the crisp blue folder.

She opened it, and an old wallet-sized photo of Kaleb stared up at her. It had been years since she had seen him look like he did in that picture. The roots of his blond curly hair peeked out from the black dye that matched the black eyeliner and black clothes he once favored.

Alice scanned the file, not that there was anything inside it that she didn't already know or couldn't have guessed.

Name: Kaleb "Rabbit" White
Birthdate: March 23, XXXX
Height: 6'3"
Weight: 180 lbs.
Father: Joseph White, Red Queen Inc.
Mother: Isabella Button, missing and presumed dead
Siblings: Sgt. Jacob P. Button, retired; Agent Markus White, FBI

Alice flipped through the folder, each page covered with blacked-out lines, maybe one or two words visible per page.

"Why are you giving me this?" Alice asked. "I already know everything here. At least what I can read."

DeeDee and Linc ignored her question. DeeDee reached for Alice's hands, and Alice flinched. There was an unspoken exchange between DeeDee and Linc before DeeDee pulled away.

Linc dropped into his drawl. "Alice, we need something from you."

She raised an eyebrow. *Is he really trying to charm me like one of the harem girls that twitter around him and his brother?*

"Lincoln Sanchez, you know that little accent of yours never worked on me. What do you want?"

Linc half smiled, half grimaced. "WonderLand. It's been released. Again."

Alice's stomach dropped as she remembered the theater and the day that turned her world into a living nightmare. She still couldn't smell popcorn without the memory of blood hanging in the air around her as the people in the theater lost their minds and lives. She lost control that day. It wasn't the first time, but it was the last. It was too much of a risk now that WonderLand was running through her veins.

Her vision flickered.

No, absolutely not. Kaleb wouldn't be involved in a cover-up. The only person with the virus was Jackson. They were lying.

Besides, if there were more victims, there would have been something on the news about a mysterious virus. Like last time. She reassured herself, but something in the back of her mind told her this was a lie.

Alice met DeeDee's eyes, not wanting to see the pity she was sure was in Linc's eyes. In an almost whisper, she asked, "Where?"

DeeDee stared down at the table, pulling on a strand of her long hair. "Red Queen Inc."

Alice was confused. There are security protocols; Dr. Turtle and Reid had shown Alice the security protocols on her first visit to Red Queen. Anyone in a room would be locked in until the virus had been cleaned from the building through the giant fans in Dr. Turtle's lab.

Though technically the virus should have been destroyed, no matter what happened, the protocols would take care of whatever the scientist had been working on.

"Okay?" she asked, knowing there had to be more to it.

Linc exchanged a look with DeeDee, then cleared his throat. "We think Kaleb may have gone into Red Queen Inc. We need you to get inside and bring him—"

"And get the cure," DeeDee added.

Linc continued. "Here."

CHAPTER 13

Kaleb pushed the red button, and in the distance, a large fan kicked on to send the rolling smoke somewhere else, away from Red Queen Inc. In time, the building would be free of the virus, but he wasn't sure how many people would suffer before then.

The door needed to be sealed off. He had seen the just-in-case look in his father's eyes when Joseph gave him the tape.

He watched Dr. Turtle pace back and forth in front of the security monitors, stopping every few minutes to look at a screen and mutter, "How could this happen? I was so close."

Worthless idiot, Kaleb thought as he taped the small cracks of the gray door. He wasn't sure if it would do anything. It had never been clear how the virus spread, but he knew if Joseph was worried, it was best to do as he said, especially when it came to the virus.

Kaleb thought about tracking Joseph's progress through the building using the security monitors. He wasn't sure if he wanted his father to make it to Ms. Redding or not.

It would be ironic if her own virus killed her.

A scream filled the hall outside the door. Dr. Turtle stopped pacing and pressed something on the monitor's control panel, bringing up the view outside the door. The woman with the long blonde hair he'd seen earlier passed the camera. Her lab coat was torn, her face was covered in crescent-shaped scratches, and she was missing a shoe.

The pink smoke moved across the floor in both directions, inching closer and closer, trapping her. Her fist slammed into the closed entrance.

Kaleb watched in horror as pink tendrils of smoke moved up her legs. He looked toward the door. *I could open it, try to save her. It would take a few minutes to override the system.*

He looked at the screen; the smoke had made its way to her stomach. *Would it be enough time?*

Kaleb took a step toward the control panel, his hands hovering over the keyboard.

The infectious cloud washed over her, consuming her, the blue-gray of her eyes disappearing into a sea of pink. *It's too late. Another death to add to my crimes.*

A loud thud against the door moved Kaleb's attention from the monitors to the door. Pink wisps of smoke floated into the room through the exposed hinges.

"Shit."

Kaleb grabbed the duct tape and ran to the door.

"Turtle," he called out to the doctor, who didn't look up from the notebook. His pen moved across the pages in a feverish frenzy. Kaleb had hoped Turtle would help; he should have known better.

The sound of duct tape coming off the roll filled the room.

Of all the people to be trapped with, I have Dr. Turtle. Useless, self-absorbed. Kaleb pushed the tape to the exposed hinges. He looked back at the doctor, still watching the screens and taking notes.

Kaleb rolled his eyes. *Of course, he would be studying the dying, leaving me to protect both of us.*

He turned around, bending over to cover the crack beneath the door and tearing a piece of tape from the roll with his teeth. He smashed the sticky side onto the door without looking. *How did I get myself into this? If I had just ignored my phone.*

Something tickled Kaleb's skin. It reminded him of tiny spider legs crawling their way up his arm. He looked down.

Smoke wound itself around his uncovered fingers, leaving a powdery residue on his exposed hand. He pulled it away from the open crack of the door, wiping it on his jeans. *How much of this pink death cloud needs to touch me before I'm infected?*

"Everything okay?" Dr. Turtle asked.

Kaleb only nodded. He thought about asking Dr. Turtle how much it would take to infect someone, but the look on the doctor's face told Kaleb that would be a bad idea. He would end up another "volunteer" in the doctor's lab.

Dr. Turtle sat down in one of the rolling chairs and studied Kaleb as if trying to decide something. "You could still live a normal life, with my help, of course." Dr. Turtle pushed the other rolling chair toward Kaleb. "You were exposed to the cloud."

Kaleb ran his hands through his hair. *Do I pretend I don't know what he's talking about or...?* "You saw that?"

"Of course."

Kaleb clasped the back of the chair, his knuckles bright white against the black fabric. "How long before I show symptoms?"

"I'm not sure." Dr. Turtle riffled through his notebook. "You seem to have control over your emotions like Alice, but do you have the same training as she did?"

Wait, what? Alice wasn't infected, was she? Kaleb tried to understand what he'd heard. *She never said she was immune. Only that she'd been exposed to WonderLand.*

"Haven't you ever wondered why Alice shows very little emotion?" Dr. Turtle asked, not looking for an answer. "What is it you all call it? Oh yes, WonderLand. Humm, how best to explain it to you so you'll understand? WonderLand tells the brain to shut down everything but those things that cause anger. It's actually quite fascinating how the emotion consumes a person."

He would think it was fascinating, Kaleb thought as he plopped down in the chair across from the doctor.

"Alice had already been working with her mother on controlling that particular emotion," Dr. Turtle continued. "I suspect it's why Elizabeth was able to keep a bit of herself in the end. Not many people can experience that level of anger and not lose their minds." Dr. Turtle looked up at the security monitors, making notes. "Though this batch seems to be working a bit differently from the others. Not sure why."

Kaleb swallowed the bile rising in his throat. *I can't believe this.* "You're telling me Alice is currently infected with WonderLand."

"Of course." Dr. Turtle turned to Kaleb. "She didn't tell you? I thought maybe she had. Alice and I talked about whether or not it would be a good idea." He shrugged. "I thought it was. Reid had already jeopardized my work because of Alice. I guess I was hoping if Alice told you, I'd get my thumb drive back."

Kaleb shrugged.

So, Turtle knew and hadn't said anything. Alice is infected. How did I not see it? And the Task Force. What else had I missed?

A loud thump sounded at the door behind Kaleb, followed by a furious pounding. Kaleb pulled the chair closer to the panel of security monitors, looking for the screen that would show the door outside.

It could be Joseph or the woman I left to die.

He pushed the images of the pink cloud consuming her aside. *It's not my fault. I didn't release the virus.*

Kaleb typed in the command to bring up the view of the security door. A pink film covered the camera, giving the world outside a rose-colored view. A bulky blond in a black hazmat suit looked up at the camera, his eyes shimmering. It was Gryff.

His meaty fist hit the thick gray door again, and he screamed at the camera. Kaleb debated opening the door.

I'm already exposed.

He looked over at Turtle, who was back to watching the virus progress through the building on one of the other screens.

Turtle hasn't been exposed. Though it would serve him right, a victim of his own creation. Kaleb shook his head. *No, he might be an unfeeling jerk, but he is the only one who can help.* He looked at the screen one last time, not wanting to watch as Gryff lost his mind.

Something in Gryff's right hand caught Kaleb's attention, the fluorescent lights glinting off the sleek silver cylinder. Gryff turned from the camera, his back against the door, arm raised, pointing down the hall. He aimed at something off camera, and a shot rang out. With a pop, the door swung open, letting the Infected in.

Gryff backed into the room, his gun pointed into the hall.

The pink smoke had disappeared in the short time Turtle had been explaining, but the residue left behind swirled around Gryff's feet.

Kaleb watched as the blonde tech in a torn lab coat stumbled into the room, dark red blood dripping from her nose and eyes.

Why isn't he shooting her? Kaleb thought, before realizing it was Martha, Gryff's wife.

Gryff stumbled backward, and Martha moved closer, her hand reaching for him. "Please," Gryff begged, "you have to fight it."

Martha lunged at him, pushing Gryff to the floor.

The gun hit the ground, skirting toward Kaleb's foot.

He looked down at the weapon and back at Martha. *How long before I do the same thing to the people I love?*

Dr. Turtle moved from the screens to stand next to Kaleb. He had a gun in his hand pointed at Martha. *Where did he get a gun?*

Dr. Turtle pulled the trigger, leaving the smell of gunpowder hanging in the air around them while Martha's body crumpled in a heap of bone and flesh on the floor.

Gryff screamed out, pulling her into his arms.

Martha's lifeless eyes stared at him, fresh blood sliding from the wound in the center of her forehead.

Kaleb looked to Gryff cradling his wife in his arms and wailing, trying to process what happened. It was one thing to see it on screen; the terrible gut-twisting guilt and fear that settled in his stomach now made him want to retch. He raced for a nearby garbage can, kicking the gun Gryff dropped across the floor.

A new thought crossed his mind. *What if Gryff got a hold of his gun?*

Kaleb bent down to grab the weapon. Grief made people do horrible things, and given that Gryff was already unpleasant on a good day, Kaleb could only imagine what he might do now that his wife was dead. Add that to the fact he was most likely infected, and Kaleb thought it best the man didn't have a weapon.

He wasn't sure how—the man should have been consumed by his grief—but Gryff somehow shuffled to his feet in time to tear the weapon from Kaleb's hands, causing Kaleb to stumble back.

The cold steel of Gryff's gun pressed into Kaleb's skull.

"You have two choices," Gryff started. "Either help me find a way out of this hellhole or..." Gryff pushed the gun further into Kaleb's temple, causing him to wince in pain. "We can add your death to today's tally."

Kaleb looked at the security screens.

The virus had taken control of the building, and if Turtle was telling the truth, before long, it would take Kaleb too. He opened his mouth to tell Gryff to go to hell, but a movement on the screen monitoring the tunnel entrance caught his eye.

Someone was trying to get in.

A woman with long blonde hair and dark-rimmed glasses moved down the ladder, stopping every few steps to catch her breath. It looked like she was...counting.

Kaleb remembered the text message his father showed him. **Package on its way.**

Alice jumped from the ladder, missing the last few rungs. No. She should be halfway to starting a new life, Markus keeping her safe. Not here. Not now.

She looked into the camera, her familiar blue-green eyes sending a flash of fear through him. *Maybe Alice doesn't know the code,* he told himself moments before she started the game that would open the electronic locks, even during an outbreak.

Kaleb ground his teeth. He was going to kill his brother if they got out of here alive.

"I'll help you."

Chapter 14

Alice's eyes moved up the bright white brick cylinder of the useless lighthouse. It was useless since it was in the middle of a desert in a landlocked state. It turned out to be the back entrance to Red Queen Inc.

She looked at the night sky. The stars gave her comfort and reminded Alice of better days, of cold nights around a firepit telling ghost stories and making s'mores with her brothers.

She adjusted the long hair of the blonde wig she wore. Strands of hair clung to the thick-rimmed black glasses that would record her every move, reminding Alice of why she liked to keep her hair short.

The blonde wig was Linc's idea; he thought it would be better if she weren't recognized. *Maybe he was right*, even if the long hair made Alice feel vulnerable. The last time it had been this length, a madman had dragged her around by it. She still couldn't believe Linc and DeeDee had convinced her to go into Red Queen. She almost turned around, but the thought that Kaleb might be in there pushed her forward. *He needs my help. I can't let him go through this alone. Not when there might be a cure.*

The small wood-slatted door on the outside of the lighthouse opened without a sound. Alice looked around for anyone who might try to follow, but she was alone. Alice ducked into the building.

She stood inside a circular room. No stairs, only dirt and stone. Alice had expected as much, but it still unnerved her.

She stepped into the center of the room to the metal grate DeeDee had told her would lead into the lower floors of Red Queen, though she'd left out that it was in the shape of a heart.

Alice rolled her eyes. *What else would it be?*

She lifted the grate and stepped onto the first rung of the metal ladder, entering the dark hole of death. With each step down the ladder, she waited to hear a groan and clink as the gate above crashed closed, trapping her inside.

Alice gripped the cold steel of the ladder, frozen in place, the darkness intensifying the fear of the walls crumbling around her that crept its way into her every thought.

Almost as if he'd been reading Alice's thoughts, Linc's gravel voice moved through her earpiece. "Twelve rungs until the bottom, three steps to the door."

Alice pressed her forehead to the cool bar and took a calming breath. *I can do this.*

"The code is yellow," Linc said.

"Okay." *Whatever that was supposed to mean.*

The smell of wet earth filled her lungs; with each step, she remembered how much she hated enclosed spaces.

Alice thought she could see the walls moving closer to her. Linc's voice buzzed in her ear. "There should be a little black box."

On the third step down, she wiped away the sweat that dripped into her eyes. At five she wished she had brought a flashlight. Then she reminded herself she was almost done, and at eleven she missed the rung and fell to the ground with a *thunk* and a lot of dust.

Alice took a couple of shaky breaths, her lungs struggling to get enough air. *I'm fine.* She looked around, trying to get her bearings, as much as she could in the dark. *Just a few more steps, then I'm inside. With the Infected. How long before... Stop, you're not going there.*

A thin bright light showed a few inches in front of her. Alice ran her fingers around the outline for the door, looking for the little black box. Her hand brushed up against the hard metal and a soft keypad that lit up with her touch. Red, green, blue, and yellow lights moved in a repeating pattern three times before the words **YOUR TURN** moved across the little screen above the keys.

Alice touched her ear to activate her mouthpiece so she could ask Linc what the code was, but the earpiece was gone.

It must've fallen out when I fell.

Alice spent a few minutes trying to find it, but even with the light from the keypad, it was too dark to see. She looked up at where she assumed the hole was, trying to remember.

Linc said something about the color yellow.

She stared at the keypad, the light flashing in a repeating multicolored pattern.

Yellow is the code.

Alice pressed down on the key that changed yellow, hoping she understood Linc's cryptic message. A sliver of silver light skirted across the dirt floor as a metal door slid up a few inches from the ground, bringing with it the fluorescent light of her escape.

A wave of relief washed over her, but she wasn't done. There had been a sequence, and she was only half paying attention when it moved across the keys, but she was worried about the missing earpiece. Her hand hovered over the keypad. *Was it the bottom right or left?*

Bottom right. Maybe. Alice pressed the key on the bottom right, and the door slid open a few inches more. More confident this time, Alice pressed the top right.

The door slid shut, plunging her back into darkness.

TWO TRIES LEFT moved across the screen, and the pattern started again, but this time it was faster. Alice watched: top left, bottom right, center, middle right, bottom right, and bottom left was all she could memorize before the words **YOUR TURN** lit the room. She hoped it would be enough.

Top left. The door moved an inch. Bottom right. A few more inches. Center and middle right. She could almost fit through the opening now. Bottom center. The door slid closed, and the room was plunged into darkness.

LAST CHANCE written in bold letters skipped across the screen, mocking her. At least that's how she felt.

The keys lit up again, but not only was the sequence faster this time, it was twice as long. Knowing she couldn't remember it all, Alice concentrated on only the first five, hoping the door would open wide enough that she could crawl through before it slammed shut.

Top left, bottom right, center, middle right, bottom right.

With shaky hands, Alice typed in what she could remember. With each button, the door moved up a bit more. When it was a quarter of the way open, Alice dropped to her knees and crawled under the small opening, dirt crunching under her palms.

Her heart pounded in her ears as her hand met the cold linoleum floor of the room behind the door. *Almost there.*

Alice looked around her while the door hovered above like a guillotine threatening to cut her in half. All she saw was a bright white light.

She pulled her feet into the room moments before the door slammed shut. She stood on shaking legs, dusting the red dirt from her pants, waiting for her eyes to adjust to the bright fluorescent lights.

The room was bigger than she expected. One wall was lined with white lab coats, the heart emblem of Red Queen Inc. stitched on the pockets, the other with the red jackets worn by security. There was a gold doorknob sticking out from a blank white wall.

Alice picked up one of the lab coats and turned around. The door she'd come in through had been replaced by a full-length mirror and it was sealed shut. At first, she was startled by her reflection, having forgotten about the wig and glasses, but she was glad to see they hadn't fallen off.

She must have stood there too long because the lens in the glasses changed to blink blue, reminding Alice the people on the Task Force were watching. She adjusted the wig, making sure there was no hint of her dark hair, and pushed aside the bangs so she could see. She smiled, took a deep breath, turned around, and twisted the doorknob attached to the wall behind her then stepped into a long gray hallway.

Her sneakers squeaked on the freshly waxed floor, adding to the dread that settled in her stomach.

Alice walked past the silver doors of the disabled elevator on her way to the security desk. Overhead lights flicked on every few steps, adding to her fear. Linc's words played through her mind. *You don't react to the strange. That's an asset.*

The name badge DeeDee gave her bounced against her chest when she turned the corner. They weren't sure how far the virus had spread, and this badge could get Alice anywhere she needed to go.

Alice pulled on the name tag, trying to read the name, anything to prevent her from going further. If the virus had gotten this far, one of two things would be waiting for her when she turned the corner: an empty desk or carnage. An empty desk meant the men behind it were already dead.

I shouldn't be here. What if I lose control? The virus, it's always there, waiting. She looked back the way she came and sighed. *There's no way out. Not until I finish the mission. Why did I agree to do this?*

The end tables that ordinarily lined the walls of the waiting room, as well as a few lab tables from somewhere deep inside the building, were lined up end to end and covered with colored paper. Coffee cups and paper were scattered across the table's surface. The floor was littered with coffee grounds, paper clips, staples, and rubber bands. Loud snoring came from under the table, but no security guards sat at the main desk. The room was empty except for whoever was asleep under the table.

Alice moved behind the security desk, trying not to disturb the sleeping form. Her hand hovered over the red button that would open the door that led into the labs of Red Queen Inc. *This is it; there's no going back.* Her hand brushed the top of the button when she heard the squeak of an office chair and someone behind her saying, "Beep beep." Alice turned toward the beeping. Alice knew the big man in a red security jacket. Madison. He knelt backward on a big black office chair, one leg pressed against the back and the other pushing him forward. His arms were raised above his head with a... cardboard sword?

The two swinging doors at the end of the reception area swung open. Harrison, the second guard, came through the double doors with a matching sword, also on a rolling office chair. He screamed, "For Narnia," and barreled toward Madison.

Alice watched as the two chairs collided with a clash. She held her breath, waiting for one or both men to lash out and rip the other apart. But they lay on the floor laughing, a heap of arms, legs, and cardboard swords.

She looked down at the two men who obviously were infected with something, but it wasn't WonderLand. On her previous visits to Red Queen Inc., the security guards had been all business. Never once had she seen them crack a smile. *They're acting like schoolchildren.*

"Oh, look a guest." Harrison kicked Madison. "Come join us for a cup of coffee," he said to Alice.

Madison rolled onto his stomach and looked up at Alice with bloodshot eyes. "Please do." He grinned. "I will make you the most fantastic hat."

Alice looked at the doors and back to the red button, not sure what was going on and how they would react if she tried to leave. *Best to play along.*

Spreading her lips into her best everything-is-great smile, she said, "Sounds like fun."

Harrison jumped up and down and clapped his hands, causing his thick black glasses to slide down his nose. "Yay! You will love it."

They each grabbed one of Alice's arms and guided her to a fluffy armchair.

Harrison, sitting in the empty folding chair next to her, picked up a coffee mug with red lipstick on the rim. It said, **Let's just agree**

that I'm right. He smiled at her before going through a paper box sitting on a chair next to him.

"We have French roast, Italian roast, light, and dark." He threw a bag on the floor. "Yuck, decaf. No decaf."

A deep, sleepy voice that Alice thought sounded a lot like Tom came from under the table. "Don't forget about the tea," he said.

"*No*. No tea. Leaf water. Yuck." Harrison took the cup and an armful of coffee bags and disappeared behind the double doors.

Madison sat down in a maroon plastic chair in front of Alice and hummed as he folded multicolored paper into flowers and cranes. Alice watched him, trying to figure out what to do. This was not what she expected. There should be blood, death, screams of agonizing pain, not insanity—well, not this kind anyway.

Harrison returned with coffee and plopped it down in front of her, causing the sludgy brew to splash onto the table. Alice looked at the dark gooey spot and knew there was something other than coffee in the cup. Harrison watched Alice.

I can't drink this.

Alice put the cup near her lips, careful not to touch the lipstick marks. The smell of coffee, chocolate, and something else she couldn't quite place assaulted her nose, causing her stomach to roll.

Harrison cleared his throat. He was still waiting for her to take a drink. Afraid of what might happen if she didn't, Alice pretended to take a sip. She put the cup down on the table, careful not to spill the toxic brew on her hand.

"Excellent," she said, a forced smile on her lips.

Harrison smiled back with a too-big grin. "Of course it is. I'm an amazing cook."

There's no way I'll be eating or drinking anything in this place. "What happened here?" she asked.

"Party," Madison answered. "Only one came."

A grumble sounded under the table. "You didn't send out invitations."

"That's right." Madison held a paper crane in one hand and a flower in the other, his fingers moving skillfully, weaving paper and paper clip together. "I forgot." He held out his creation to Alice.

She turned it over in her hand, amazed at the craftsmanship. An idea formed in her mind.

"I bet if I showed the people your hat, they would want to come." Alice looked at the double doors. "I could go and show them."

Madison shook his head. "No one can go through those doors except Harrison and Tom."

Alice looked at the boots sticking out from under the table. *So it is Tom sleeping under the table.*

"Oh, and Alice," Harrison said through a mouth full of cookies. "She can always go in."

Alice looked between the two men at the table, both engrossed in a meaningless task. "Why?"

"Orders."

"Whose orders?" she asked.

Madison looked up from his paper folding to stare at Alice. His eyes shimmered in the light as he looked her over. With each blink, the fog that held him captive lifted. His dark eyes focused on her. "Alice?" he whispered.

She nodded.

"You shouldn't be here."

She smiled a slight smile, letting her sadness peek through. "I know, but I need to find something."

She watched him, the internal argument he was having with himself on his face. *What am I going to do if he doesn't let me pass?*

His face scrunched up in frustration before a sad, understanding smile crossed his lips. "Okay, I'll let you in."

Alice placed her hand on his too-warm hand. "Thank you."

Madison stood up, his shoulders slumped and feet shuffling as he walked behind the security desk. He raised his hand above the red button that would open the door. He looked over at Harrison, who was searching through bags of coffee, and for a moment it looked like he wasn't going to let her through, but then a buzz filled the room, and the double doors opened with a *whoosh.*

Alice stood up, careful not to trip over the sleeping Tom's feet, and walked across the room to the open doors. She stopped at the threshold; streaks of red littered the floor ahead. A weird sense of relief underlined with dread came over her. This was what she expected.

Memories of the theater flickered in her mind. Alice took a deep breath, ready to count. *I'm fine.* She shuffled forward a few steps, dread settling into her stomach.

Flashes of that day surfaced: sticky red popcorn on the floor, a cloud of fine pink dust covering the room. Specks of red on silver stars against a blue backdrop. *How long had I sat with my knees to my chest, staring at those stars before they found me? This is a bad idea.*

Madison's throaty voice broke through Alice's thoughts. "Have I gone mad?"

Alice tried to clear her mind before answering. *One, two, three.* She turned to face Madison. *Four, five...* She met his big eyes. "I'm afraid so."

A frown appeared on his face.

"But all the best people are," she assured him.

Alice took a step backward into the next room, listening for anyone who might come up behind her as she went. It was the only way she could move forward. She couldn't face what was coming, not yet. Madison watched her from the security desk, a walkie in his hand and the frown still on his lips. The doors closed with a swish.

There's no turning back now. Time to face my fear and find a cure.

CHAPTER 15

Kaleb was handcuffed to the black rolling chair, again. This time it was to keep him in one place while they waited for the virus to clear out of the building. Gryff didn't want Kaleb leaving him locked in the building when the time came to escape. *Not that I have any idea how to get us out of here.*

Gryff and Dr. Turtle stood near the broken door, conversing in low tones. It seemed like they were arguing about something.

Thankful, not for the first time, that Red Queen Inc. had a state-of-the-art security system, Kaleb tracked Alice's movements through the building on the screen. *At least they haven't noticed her yet.*

Alice walked down an empty hall toward the waiting room, and Kaleb remembered seeing Madison clocking in this morning. *Had he survived the initial outbreak?*

A bunch of tables lined the center of the waiting room, reminding Kaleb of Thanksgivings and making room for unexpected guests. A dark-haired man walked into the room, his head down. Kaleb moved closer to the screen; something about the man bothered him.

The man moved around the room, keeping his face from the view of the camera. Kaleb knew with a few keystrokes he could change the camera view to capture the guy's face. *Not that knowing who it is will help Alice.*

Kaleb looked back at Gryff and Turtle, who were still arguing in front of the open door. He turned back to the screen in time to see Tom staring into the camera.

Tom climbed under the table, his booted feet sticking out from underneath. Kaleb's heart sped up. Alice was about to walk into that room. Tom had done unspeakable things for a fix, and now Alice was going to be trapped in that waiting room with him.

Dr. Turtle's stuttered voice moved through the room. "I c-c-can't."

Gryff moved toward Kaleb, gun raised. Kaleb rose from his chair, ready to use the flimsy thing as a weapon. *Honestly, who handcuffs someone to a rolling chair?*

A glint of a smile moved across Gryff's lips. His shimmering eyes focused on Kaleb, whispered words moving across his lips.

Kaleb stared at the barrel of the gun, the circular cylinder playing with his darkest fears, the threat of a simple piece of metal freezing his thoughts. He was powerless. Suddenly, he was once again a child hidden away in his parent's closet listening to the tortured screams of his mother.

Madison's voice cracked over a nearby walkie. "Code Blue." It was the phrase used by security to let Ms. Redding know Alice was in the building.

Gryff looked around the room, confusion plain on his face. He still pointed the gun at Kaleb, but with less resolve. Kaleb knew he should take advantage of this moment, but he was still stuck in his past.

Dr. Turtle moved between them and picked up the walkie on the desk. "Repeat."

"Code Blue."

Alice. They know she's here.

Kaleb looked at the monitors over Dr. Turtle's shoulder, his heart beating in his ears as he watched Alice leave the waiting room and step into the empty lab. The walls were stained red with blood from an earlier incident. He watched Alice and noticed her eyes never focused on the carnage.

Dr. Turtle examined the screens and then lifted the walkie to his mouth. "Location."

Kaleb looked at Turtle, astonished he hadn't recognized Alice. Her short dark hair covered by a blonde wig had actually hidden her identity.

Madison's voice crackled through the air. "East entrance."

Dr. Turtle studied the screen for a moment before turning to Kaleb. "If I get you out of this room, can you bring her to me?"

Kaleb thought about telling him no. Something in the doctor's eyes gave Kaleb the impression she would be better off in Red Queen Inc. alone than anywhere near Dr. Turtle.

"What are you doing?" Gryff asked.

Dr. Turtle turned to Gryff with his hand out, waiting for something to be dropped in it. "If Alice got in, then she can get out, and Kaleb is our best bet in getting that information. Alice trusts him." Dr. Turtle turned to face Kaleb. "Right?"

"Right." *At least for now.*

Gryff turned to Kaleb and asked, "What's to stop you from leaving with Alice?"

"You said it yourself." Kaleb shrugged. "The safest place to wait out the most violent of the Infected is here."

Now that the pink infection cloud had settled into a fine dust, the only thing they needed to worry about was the Infected getting in.

That must have been the right answer because Gryff moved past Dr. Turtle and uncuffed Kaleb. He stood up, rubbed his wrists, and moved across the room toward the open door. "I shouldn't be more than twenty minutes. Once I'm gone, block the door."

Dr. Turtle nodded.

Kaleb stepped into the hall and waited for the door to close behind him. *I don't need Gryff to shoot me in the back,* he thought. Once he was sure the door was not only closed but blocked, Kaleb ran.

He ran through the maze of halls, slipping on pink dust, praying not to run into anybody, and wishing he had some kind of weapon. *How long before someone recognizes Alice? What will happen if they do? What if Tom recognizes her? Will he lose control? Will she?*

The bright lights of the lab came into view. Kaleb picked up speed, his heart pounding in his ears, pushing him forward.

A gloved hand clasped Kaleb's arm and pulled him to a stop. He tried to pull free, but the grip tightened. Kaleb turned and slugged the person who held him, but he missed. His fist sank into the gray plaster wall, littering the floor with pink-and-white dust.

"Stop fighting. I'm trying to help you."

Kaleb met Ryan's smiling face, doubting him immediately. "Then why attack me?"

"I didn't attack you. You attacked me." Ryan let go of Kaleb's arm. "Both now, and in the parking lot."

"How do I know you aren't—"

Ryan cut him off. "The Thavasi is out of my system, and I wasn't here when WonderLand was released. As long as I don't touch the pink crap littering the floor, I'll be fine."

"Why are you here? How did you get in?"

Ryan peeked his head down the hall before explaining. "When the Task Force lost contact with Alice, they wanted to write her off, but Linc wouldn't do that. He sent me here to find her and get her out."

Ryan pulled a pink glitter phone from his pocket. Kaleb recognized it immediately, even without the pig snout covering the camera lens. Kit had a thing for pigs. *Did that mean Marci was helping Ryan?*

"Why would you risk your life to save Alice?" Kaleb asked.

Ryan slipped the phone back into his front pocket. "It's my fault she's here, that you're here. If I hadn't stopped you..." Ryan moved closer to the hallway. "We'll have to pick this up later."

A group of people walked past them toward the large open room

Kaleb had last seen Alice in. He no longer cared how or even why Ryan was there. All he cared about was Alice.

Ryan turned to Kaleb with a smile that showed all his teeth and said, "Time to go."

CHAPTER 16

Alice scanned the large room, looking for the doctors and lab students who, on a normal day, would be running from patient to patient. The nurses' station in the center was empty, as well as the beds surrounded by white curtains hung on tracks that lined the walls. She couldn't see them from where she stood, but Alice knew the curtains had little red hearts on them.

A blood trail led to the furthest part of the room, the curtains drawn around it. She knew there could be horrors she didn't want to see behind them, but she needed to know if someone was there.

She'd already ignored the blood-spattered walls. Did she want to take the chance the person who belonged to that blood was behind that curtain? What if they were hurt? Or worse, violent?

Or.

What if it's Kaleb? She stopped, looked around the room, and took a couple of steps.

If this is the virus, it's different this time. Madison and Harrison had a childlike craziness to them, not the murderous rage she'd expected.

Alice wiped her hands on her jeans. Maybe the person behind the curtain wouldn't be violent. Her hand settled on the curtain.

Scrrrrrap.

A tall skinny kid with red hair and acne was bent over a metal bucket, sponge hovering over soapy water. He dunked the cloth into the water and caused the bucket to move across the floor making the scraping noise she'd heard before. Red-and-pink bubbles sloshed onto the floor, and Alice hoped the color was from soap but suspected it was blood. His eyes met hers, and she recognized him, even with the red smear on his face. It was the sweet, if not a bit flirty, intern who showed up at all her appointments.

"Shawn?"

He stood, a big, yellow sponge in his hand. "The walls, they're red. The Queen, she wants them white." A pink streak ran down the wall where he'd wiped his sponge. "Everything shiny and clean, just like new."

Alice took a step closer to him. *Who was the Queen? Reid?* It was the only person she could think of who would call herself that. "Have you seen the Queen?"

He pushed the bucket across the floor and closer to Alice. "Shiny and clean."

Clack.

A gunshot echoed through the hall, causing Alice to knock over the bucket of not-so-clean water. She scanned the room, trying to decide how close the shooter was and whether she should find somewhere to hide. If she did hide, she would need to take Shawn with her; she couldn't leave him behind.

Alice turned to where he had been cleaning the wall. Shawn was on the floor, mopping up the spilled water with his stomach. The water changed the once-white lab coat he was wearing pink. He looked up at Alice with a wide smile on his face.

Clack.

Another shot rang out. Two people came rushing into the room from a back hall, wearing the same lab coats as her and Shawn. They had black gas masks hanging around their necks like the ones she'd seen in the movies that took place during World War II.

"The Queen is coming," they yelled as they rushed past Alice, acting as if she didn't exist. They grabbed Shawn's arms and legs and pushed him back and forth like a mop, cleaning the spilled water.

"What are you doing?" she asked, knowing she should leave, but her curiosity got the better of her.

One of the guys holding Shawn's legs looked at Alice through the shield of the gas mask. "None of your business."

Alice looked at the hall. How long did she have until the Queen showed up? And did she want to be here when she did?

Shawn squealed as the two men pushing him across the floor started to argue.

"You're hurting him."

"No, you are."

"How am I hurting him?"

They dropped his limbs and started to circle each other, fists up in cartoon fashion, ready to fight. Frustrated, Alice's vision started flickering to black and white. If she didn't leave these people to their nonsense soon, she'd be unable to control herself, and she would make the blood on the walls theirs. *I can't save everyone. Infected or not.*

Alice turned to leave, but Reid and Kaleb's dad, Joe, blocked her path. Both were armed and smelled of smoke. A large group of people stomped into the room behind them. Reid walked past Joe, ignoring Alice, and approached the three men who now lay cowering on the floor.

"Who are"—Reid kicked Shawn, and he howled—"they?"

Joe moved to stand next to Reid. "Nobodies, Your Majesty," he said.

A warm hand clutched Alice's wrist, and she suppressed a scream as she was tugged closer. Her heart kicked up. Warm breath moved across her ear, whispering words across her senses. "It's me."

Alice would know that voice anywhere. She looked up. Kaleb's blue eyes, sparkling with intelligence, not virus, stared down at her. He was alive.

He must have seen something in her reaction because he whispered, "I'm not infected."

She let out a heavy sigh of relief, and Reid turned toward them, a familiar shimmer in her eyes. It was the same shimmer Alice saw in the mirror every day. Cold dread ran through her veins. Kaleb may not have been infected, but Reid was, and Alice had somehow shined a light on their presence.

Reid turned back to the men on the floor but not before giving Alice a look that said, "I'll deal with you later."

She ordered the men on the ground to their feet. They did this standing-bowing thing that made them look like bobbing ducks, water dripping into a puddle at their feet.

Reid turned to Alice. "Who are they?"

Alice shrugged. She didn't know what to say.

She knew Shawn, but not the other two. What if her answer got them killed? Sure, they were infected, but if what DeeDee said was true, there was a cure, and it was somewhere in this building.

"Who are you?" Reid asked Alice.

A warm hand grabbed her other wrist, but unlike Kaleb, this grip was tight, and Alice knew it would leave a bruise. She looked down at the hand that held her other arm. It was freckled. *Ryan? How had he gotten here? DeeDee told me they'd had him detained.*

"This is..." Ryan started, but Kaleb cut him off.

"Her name badge says Martha, and she's a lab student."

Ryan smiled his big white toothy grin at the two of them before turning to Reid. "She would make a great addition to our game."

Alice held her breath as Reid looked her over. "Yes."

"What about the others?" Joe asked, motioning to Shawn and his friends.

A wicked smile spread across Reid's face. She handed Ryan a gun. "Shoot them."

"No!" Alice hadn't meant for the word to leave her mouth, but there it was.

"Are you questioning my orders?" Reid asked.

Alice shook her head. "No, uh, Your Majesty?" She looked at Kaleb's horror-struck face. "I wanted to be the one to do it."

There was no way she was going to kill them. They were victims of the virus, like her. If she could keep Shawn and his friends away from Reid, maybe she could hide them away until she found the cure.

Kaleb mouthed, "What are you doing?"

Hoping Kaleb would understand and play along, Alice gave him her trust-me smile.

Alice pulled her arms from the man who held them, and revealing her inner villain, she strolled over to the three dripping wet men. "I know I said I didn't know them, but the truth is, I've hated them since my first day here. They treated me as nothing more than an errand girl, stealing my ideas."

She smacked one across the face, pain shooting through her hand at the contact; she didn't realize how bad it would hurt. "They think they are better than me, and why? Just because my parts aren't on the outside."

Reid smirked. "Girl after my own heart. What was your name again?"

"Martha."

Reid held her hand out to Ryan, waiting for him to give her the gun. He bypassed Reid and handed it to Alice.

Alice had never held a gun, and it weighed more than she expected. "Of course, I would like to take my time, make them suffer a bit first," she said.

Reid grinned. "Of course."

Kaleb took a step toward Alice, but his father moved in front of him. "Your Highness, I don't want to ruin your fun, but it is your turn to hide."

Reid looked at Joe and clapped her hands. "Oh yes, oh yes, we mustn't forget the game."

"We will count to fifty." He stood in front of the crowd of people. "You'll find the Queen and hide with her. The last one to find her is the loser and will be shot on sight." He looked at Reid. "Ready, set, go."

Joe pointed at a woman in a bright green business suit with matching shoes. "Count to fifty."

Kaleb clasped Alice's hand, and they took a step closer to the three men cowering in front of them. He pulled the curtain shut, leaving the larger group behind. She knew the counting would cover any noise that might come from within the semiprivacy of the curtained room.

At first, Alice didn't say anything as she tried to go over in her mind what had happened. *Would I have done it? Would I have killed them?*

"Ace."

Alice looked at the gun, her knuckles white against the black metal. *What am I doing here?*

Kaleb moved closer and whispered, "Ace?"

The curtain moved, and Ryan stepped through the small opening. He pointed a gun at one of the men on the floor.

"What are you doing?" Kaleb demanded.

Ryan smiled his catlike smile.

The next moments happened in slow motion. Kaleb fired his gun. Alice screamed. The three men on the floor started crying. Ryan squirmed on the floor, groaning in pain. The people outside the curtain ran away, screaming.

Joe pulled the curtain open, the curtain rings scraping across the rod. "Let that be a lesson to you," he yelled.

Two more shots sounded from Kaleb's gun as he fired into the floor. Alice fell to the ground with her hands over her head and watched Kaleb whisper something to Shawn. He and the other two lay down in awkward positions on the floor as if they had been shot.

Kaleb helped Alice to her feet and straightened the blonde wig, which had been knocked loose on her way to the ground. His warm hand rested on her cheek. "Are you okay?"

No, she wasn't okay. He had shot someone; she had a gun in her hand and was supposed to shoot someone. Then there was all this sneaking into a place she didn't want to go, and for what? A cure that might not exist. Alice took a deep breath, trying to control her emotions. *Kaleb was safe.* "I'm fine."

Kaleb kissed her forehead. "That's my girl." He tugged her closer. "I have to check on Ryan."

Alice watched Kaleb place his fingers on Ryan's throat to check for a pulse. The curtain opened again. Joe stood in the center of the makeshift room, scanning the area. His eyes stopped on Alice. Her heart quickened. His eyes shimmered with infection.

"What happened here?" Joe asked.

Alice looked at Kaleb before saying, "He's working for..."

Kaleb interrupted her. "He's with the Duchess. I saw him with her yesterday. It's in my report."

Duchess?

Joe picked Ryan up by the collar of his shirt. That's when Alice saw the blood dripping down Ryan's arm in rivulets from a wound in his shoulder. His eyes fluttered open, not shimmering. He wasn't infected. Joe snarled at Ryan. "You have two choices: You can take this up with the Queen or me. Either way, you will lose your head."

Ryan spat in his face.

Why is he acting like this if he isn't infected?

Joe turned to his son. "I'll take care of him."

Chapter 17

Alice tried to keep track of where they were going: left, right, right, left... Not right. She was completely lost. The only thing she knew for sure was that overhead lights flashed on as they ran, highlighting the carnage around them, and that her lungs burned. She'd never run this much in her life.

Pulling her hand from Kaleb's, she used a nearby wall to hold herself up as she gulped down air, trying to forget about the metallic taste in her mouth. Kaleb kept going. She thought about calling out to him but knew nothing would come out. So she waited for him to notice she was no longer next to him and come back for her.

It didn't take long.

Alice gasped. "Why are we running?"

"I need to get you somewhere safe before..." He rubbed the back of his neck. "I've been keeping something from you."

"I know."

"How?"

"Lucky guess." Alice took a deep breath and counted to three before answering. "First, you left me unconscious in a parking lot with no memory of what happened. Then Ryan drugged me, again—or at least I think it was him; otherwise, that means you drugged me back at your place."

He opened his mouth to speak, but Alice cut him off.

"Honestly, I just can't deal with that right now. Thankfully, your little Task Force friends found me."

That wasn't quite the truth. Alice had walked into a dangerous situation without thinking. She had to be saved by the Task Force, but Kaleb didn't need to know that either.

"And now they've sent me in to find the cure." Alice pushed away from the wall. "For heaven's sake, Kaleb, this entire building is infected and has been placed on lockdown for hours."

"The Task Force sent you?"

"Of course they did. How do you think I got in here?" She pointed to the glasses. "Where do you think I got the wig and glasses? I had an earpiece so they could talk to me, but I lost it."

Kaleb moved in close to her and reached for the glasses, her only way to communicate with the Task Force. He slid them off her face, the plastic earpieces tickling her cheek. He turned them over in his hand, examining them, darkness crossing his face with each pass over the lens. After the third turn, Kaleb threw the plastic glasses onto the floor. Alice watched as the right lens popped out of the frame and skated across the tile.

"What the hell?"

He growled. "Who at the Task Force sent you?"

Alice thought about kneeing him, but when she met his eyes, she saw real fear. "Linc and DeeDee."

"Anyone else?"

"They were the only people I talked to."

He started to pace back and forth.

"What's going on here, Kaleb?"

Kaleb glanced around the empty hall. "Alice, this isn't the place or the time." He held out his hand to her. "We need to get somewhere safe."

She debated going back the way she came, forgetting this whole secret mission thing she'd gotten herself wrapped up in. *Not that I can remember how to get out of here.* She glanced down the hall that looked like all the others and sighed. "Fine, but this isn't over."

She grabbed his hand, knowing if he got ahead of her, she'd never be able to find her way out. They took a few steps, but he stopped near the glasses. Kaleb lifted his booted foot and stomped on them. The crunch of plastic and glass echoed through the halls. *What happened between Kaleb and the Task Force?*

He pulled her forward.

They ran through a few more halls before Kaleb stopped in front of a steel door. The word *security* was painted in thick black letters on it. A keycard reader hung by its wires, and the wall around it was charred black. Kaleb knocked on the door three times, and after some shuffling on the other side, the door opened.

A tall blond man stood in the doorway. He smiled at Kaleb, but then he noticed Alice, and the smile was replaced with a scowl. Kaleb turned to Alice, studying her before he pulled off the long strands of the blonde wig and freed her short brown hair.

"Just Alice," he said.

The guy looked her over again before opening the door and ushering them both through.

The door slammed shut, and the tall guy pushed a desk in front of it. Alice looked around the room, noticing one wall was lined with computer monitors.

Leaving Kaleb to his whispered conversation with the tall stranger, Alice stepped closer to the screens. Kaleb had brought her to the very place she had been looking for. Alice needed to get a better look at what was going on in Red Queen Inc., and this was the perfect place to do it.

The Infected ran from room to room, rooms that should have been locked, with makeshift weapons in their hands. A dark liquid that Alice assumed was blood covered their bodies. A few people had escaped the Infected, and many looked to be hiding among the dead. Alice's chest tightened; she'd done the same thing in the theater.

Alice moved away from the screens to Kaleb. He clasped her hand in his, and she tried to look at anything but the live video.

She hadn't noticed Dr. Alexander Turtle sitting in the corner; the man had a way of blending into the background. He nodded to her, and Alice smiled back. She liked him. He didn't make her feel like a freak when she came in for tests. Plus he seemed to be genuinely interested in her well-being. Then there was the whole keeping-her-infected-status-a-secret thing.

Kaleb turned to Alice and pointed at the tall man. "This is Gryff Maxwell."

Alice let go of Kaleb's hand to take Gryff's outstretched one. His hands were rough and calloused, but he had a warm, inviting smile.

"It's nice to finally meet you," he said.

"Gryff and Dr. Turtle are going to look after you."

She looked at the two men in the room. "Look after me?" She didn't need strangers to watch out for her; she didn't need anyone to look after her. Alice heard Gryff shuffle to the other side of the room where Dr. Turtle sat.

"You're leaving again." She growled. "At least I'm awake this time."

"Ace." He looked at the screens on the wall and pointed to the one nearest to them. Kaleb's dad had Ryan tied to a chair. Ryan's eyes were closed; if not for his heavy breaths, she would've thought he was dead. "I can't let him..." Kaleb pushed her hair behind her ears. "Do you trust me?"

She looked at him. The boy who had helped her find the way back to being a person after her mom's death. She hated it, but she knew, even with the mess that her life had become, she did trust him.

"More than I should."

He pulled her closer. "I'll be right back. I promise."

"Okay." Besides, she thought, if anyone knew if or where there was a cure, it would be Dr. Turtle, and without Kaleb hovering or Reid Redding watching, maybe she could get some answers.

Gryff appeared next to them. "Now that that's settled, Kaleb, let's get you out of here."

Kaleb led Alice to the door.

"Ace." He looked at Gryff, who was hovering nearby, and he

leaned in close to Alice. "Trust no one." He pulled Alice in and kissed her. It wasn't an all-encompassing firework kind of kiss but a quick peck. Still, he had never done anything like it before, and Alice was...well, she didn't know. Confused, maybe.

She pushed the thoughts aside and watched him leave. The steel door closed on his smiling face.

Alice turned to the other two men in the room, the weight of the gun Kaleb had slipped into her lab coat adding to her fear.

What has he gotten me into?

Chapter 18

Kaleb looked back at the gray security door.

Everything is so screwed up. I'm trapped in a building with a bunch of virus-crazed people, and the only way out depends on Ryan, who only hours before had been manic with the effects of Thavasi. If I had only gotten the phone before Joseph dragged him off. I shot Ryan. Why did I shoot Ryan?

A scream echoed down the empty hall, reminding Kaleb he needed to move. The video feed in the security office had shown that Joseph had Ryan in a small office next to the conference room. Kaleb couldn't let his father kill Ryan. He needed Ryan alive; it was the only way to get Alice out. *Marci and Linc would never have sent Ryan into this madhouse without an exit plan.*

Dr. Turtle had assured Kaleb that Gryff was fine and showed no signs of the virus. "Gryff speaks in violence," Turtle told him. Still, before leaving, Kaleb made sure Gryff understood that if anything happened to Alice, his only way out would be a slow, painful death.

The familiar *click, click, click* of Ms. Redding's heels came toward Kaleb.

Not wanting the delay of running into the Queen, Kaleb ducked into a small office to wait for her to pass.

The room held four cubicles with gold nameplates fastened outside each dividing wall. Kaleb did a quick sweep of the room, making sure he was alone. Phones dangled from their cradles, and broken picture frames littered the floor, but not a single living person occupied the room. A door nearby slammed shut, rattling the wall and disturbing the pink virus-filled dust. *Guess the lockdown didn't work on this part of the building.*

Kaleb moved further into the room, looking for somewhere to take cover. Glass crunched under his foot, and he looked down to see what he'd stepped on. A silver frame lay mangled under his boot. He picked up the picture, brushing glass from the frame. A woman with long dark curls and three boys—fourteen, ten, and four—stared up at Kaleb. The youngest, a blond boy, smiled a toothy grin at the camera, at the father he worshipped. *How is this here? It was destroyed.*

A gunshot rang out, reminding Kaleb he couldn't stand around looking at old photos. He pulled the glossy print from the confines of the broken frame, folded it in half, and slipped it into his front pocket.

The Queen's laughter echoed down the hall. She was close, and Kaleb still hadn't found a place to hide. He pushed one of the rolling chairs under the door handle—if she couldn't get in, maybe the Queen would move on—and then climbed under a desk. The corners of the picture he'd shoved in his pocket pressed into his leg. He pulled it out and turned it over in his hands, replaying the events of the last hour.

Alice was alive. When he left the security office to get her, he wasn't sure she would be that way by the time he got to her. Then Ryan... Ryan had almost told a room full of crazy gun-toting virus-infected people who she was.

Kaleb clenched his fist, crumpling the picture between his fingers. *Ryan held a gun on Alice. My Alice. That's why I shot him.*

Anger washed over Kaleb. Images of the things he wanted to do to Ryan, to the people in that room, and even to Linc for sending Alice into Red Queen Inc. played out in his head, flooding his imagination with red.

The handle of the door jiggled, pulling Kaleb back to reality.

He waited, listening. He heard only the sound of his heartbeat.

Nothing happened.

Still seeing red, he uncrumpled the photo once again. He hoped remembering better times would give him strength. A door further down the hall slammed shut. Kaleb looked at the photo, but it wasn't a picture of his family. Two pugs, one black and the other tan, stared at him. Their long pink tongues hung out of their squished faces. He turned the photo over. *This has to be a mistake. It's a picture of my family.* Kaleb's heartbeat sped up. *This isn't right.*

Kaleb stood up and tossed the picture to the floor. *No, I didn't lie to her. I'm not infected. It's the fear of being found. The fear is playing tricks on me.* He moved the chair away from the door and waited. Listening.

He heard nothing.

Kaleb turned the handle, moved into the hall, and headed toward the room he knew his father had Ryan in, trying to convince himself he hadn't seen something that wasn't there the entire way.

The door was wide open. Ryan sat in a large wooden chair, his hands fastened behind him and his head slumped back.

Kaleb was walking into a trap. There was no other explanation. Why leave a door open with a prisoner inside? *Joseph could be infected,* Kaleb reminded himself. If that was the case, he might leave the door open. *It doesn't matter. Ryan is my only hope to get Alice out.*

Kaleb moved into the room, his senses on high alert.

Blood pooled on the floor around Ryan's feet. If it weren't for his heavy breathing, Kaleb would have thought Ryan was dead. Kaleb looked around for the bright pink phone. *I need that phone.* Joseph would have emptied Ryan's pockets before torturing him.

It's not here.

There was a knife, though, sitting in the open, inches from Ryan. The fluorescent lights above highlighted its sleek body.

Kaleb looked at the knife and back at Ryan. Maybe it wasn't a trap but a test, the knife put there to tempt Kaleb. *To do what, though?* He clasped the knife in his hand. Black leather caressed his palm. Kaleb unsheathed the blade; light glinted off the silver edge, showing images of what his father had done with his weapon of choice. Torment and pain had bathed the blade in its crimson current; it pulsed red with it. Its seductive song called to Kaleb, reminding him of his distrust of Ryan.

Rabbit took a step closer to the chair, his grip so tight on the knife that its leather bonds no longer caressed but cut into his palm. His hand trembled with excitement. Or fear? Kaleb wasn't sure. All he was sure of was that he wanted Ryan to feel pain, and Rabbit wanted to be the reason why.

Silver steel shimmered into scarlet against the dark skin of Ryan's wrist. Rabbit slipped the knife between the ropes that bound him and the soft flesh of his arm.

I don't want to hurt Ryan, but he's here to kill me and Alice. Kaleb took a deep breath, trying to clear his mind. *No, Ryan doesn't want to kill us. That's not right.* He pulled the knife out.

"Kaleb?" Ryan coughed. "What are you doing?"

Kaleb took a deep breath.

I was...was I...? I almost killed him... Not killed, tortured.

He looked around the room, trying to ground himself. *I'm not Joseph. I am not a killer.*

His voice cracked when he finally spoke. "Getting you out of here." Kaleb slid the knife under the rope and cut it, careful not to cut Ryan's wrist. Then he put his shoulder under Ryan's armpit to help him to his feet.

Ryan winced, wrapping his free hand around his chest. "I don't have the phone." He groaned.

"Don't worry about it. We'll get it back."

There was no way Joseph would let me keep a phone, even if it shouldn't work in the building...

Wait. That's right. Phones don't work in the building. Kaleb adjusted his grip on Ryan, who winced.

"How does the phone work in the building?" Kaleb asked.

"Mar—"

The door, their only exit, slammed shut, and Joseph's deep voice boomed through the room. "I was wondering the same thing." Joseph stood in front of the door. He held the pink phone in his hand, the screen lighting the room in front of him. "No names in the contacts, no way to dial out, but internet access. I've never seen anything like it." He turned the screen toward himself. "Granted, I can't do much without the password." Joseph met Kaleb's eyes, the shimmer he'd seen before gone.

Kaleb glared at his father, not saying anything. He wasn't going to tell his father there was a way out. Joseph would use it to get Redding out.

His father raised an eyebrow. "Son, I thought at the very least you would try to lie to me. Some crazy story laced with bitter sarcasm."

Ryan rasped next to him. "It's a way out."

"What are you doing?" Kaleb growled at Ryan.

Ryan leaned further into Kaleb's side. "Trust me," he breathed.

Kaleb wanted to argue with Ryan, tell him whatever he planned wouldn't work. His father would see right through it.

Kaleb thought back to the picture he had thought was of his family but wasn't really, and he knew his judgment was skewed and that he might be infected. *I almost killed Ryan, and not because he had done something to hurt me or someone I cared about, but because I could.*

"Fine," Kaleb grumbled.

Ryan took a deep, rattled breath before meeting Joseph's gaze. "Sir, you don't want Kaleb here. You never did."

Joseph scoffed. "He's my son. Of course I want him here with me."

"I've..." A cough racked Ryan's body, nearly pulling him and Kaleb to the floor. Kaleb took a step back toward the chair he had helped Ryan from moments before, but Ryan stood firm. He pushed himself to his full height and stared down Joseph. "I've seen the letters, the ones you sent your wife after Dr. Elizabeth Smith—*Alice's mom*—told you what was going on here. I've seen your plan to get

Kaleb out. He was supposed to disappear the day of the last theater experiment."

"You're lying," Kaleb said. *My father would never let me go.*

Joseph took a step toward Kaleb. "I never wanted this for you. Secrets, lies, murder. No parent wants that." He ran his fingers through his hair before meeting Kaleb's gaze. "Hell, I would have done it sooner, but your mother didn't want you to live a life on the run either. She had finally found a safe place where the reach of Reid Redding and Red Queen Inc. couldn't get to her or her sons."

He knew. Kaleb breathed. "Ohio." *Why did I say that out loud? What if he finds her? Will she be safe?*

A sad smile crossed Joseph's face. "I thought your mother might have found a way to contact you." Joseph turned his back to Kaleb, his shoulders slumped. "I'm sorry, but Reid will never let Kaleb go. He knows too much. She will use every resource she has to track him down." He turned to face Kaleb. "At least if you're here, I can protect you."

"He's right." Kaleb sighed.

Not about protecting me. It's his fault I'm in this mess. Reid Redding owns people in every branch of every government and most of the criminal underground. The only reason Mom escaped was that everyone believes Isabella Button is dead.

Joseph turned around, the mask he had worn since the day they had "buried" Kaleb's mother on his face. "Put the spy back."

Kaleb helped Ryan back into the chair. *I'll have to find a different way to get Alice out.* "You could use the release of WonderLand to your advantage," Ryan said, pain marking his face with each word. "Kaleb could be among the dead."

"Reid would know," Joseph said.

Ryan smiled. "Would she? She didn't recognize Alice, and the girl was standing right in front of her."

It was true; she hadn't recognized Alice. Kaleb looked over at his father. The wheels of a plan moved behind Joseph's eyes. "How would he get out? We're in lockdown."

"The phone; it's a way out."

Joseph pulled the glitter-covered phone from his back pocket. "This pink monstrosity?"

Ryan nodded. "There's a map to an extraction point. I was supposed to use it to get...well, it doesn't matter now. Kaleb can use it to get out."

Kaleb watched Joseph study the phone, his fingers sliding over the screen. "The password."

"Pearl."

It was Kaleb's father's nickname for his wife. *How had Ryan known?* Joseph held out the phone to Kaleb. "Go."

"Are you sure?"

Joseph met Kaleb's eyes, a shimmer in his gaze. "Go now before I change my mind."

Kaleb grabbed the phone from his father's grasp and tucked it into his back pocket. He wondered whether Joseph's compassion was part of the effect of whatever ran through his veins but knew at the same time that didn't make sense. He leaned down and helped Ryan to his feet. *I'm losing my mind.*

"He stays," Joseph barked.

"What? Why?" Kaleb asked.

"You heard me."

"But..."

Ryan interrupted him. "He's right. I have to stay. It's the only way. Besides, I'll only slow you down."

Kaleb didn't feel right about leaving Ryan here with his father. "Are you sure about this?" Kaleb asked.

"I knew this was going to be a one-way trip." Ryan looked down at his bruised and bloody hands. "It's my fault you're here."

"That wasn't you. It was the Thavasi."

A sad smile crossed Ryan's lips. "Part of it was me."

Kaleb wanted to argue, but he knew Dr. Turtle's drugs didn't change you but changed the emotion you acted on.

Joseph moved closer, his shadow looming over the two men. He gripped Kaleb's arm and pulled him toward the door and into the empty hall. Joseph pulled Kaleb into a tight hug. He held Kaleb for a few seconds, neither of them saying anything. Kaleb knew this was his father saying goodbye, and he wasn't sure he was ready for it.

Joseph moved away first, going into the room without looking back. Kaleb stood in the empty hall stunned, stuck in his conflicting emotions.

The *click, click* of Ms. Redding's heels down the hall motivated him to move, but not before making a promise to himself.

Kaleb would find a way to come back and save Ryan and his father.

Chapter 19

Alice sat down in a black rolling chair next to Dr. Turtle, looking for answers. "What I know so far is that there are these designer drugs that screw with people's emotions." She looked over at Dr. Turtle. "And then there is a virus. WonderLand. It was released in the theater and now in Red Queen Inc."

Dr. Turtle interrupted. "Actually, what was in the theater is a bit different from what is in Red Queen, but not by much. Fewer people are violent, and the violence didn't last as long this time."

Alice thought about the people she'd come in contact with today. They seemed different. There was some violence, but it looked like most of it had happened before she got there. If it were the same as what was released in the theater, there would be more bodies.

Alice went on with her speech. "We'll get back to that. Let's talk about the drugs. What are they, and why make them? Is it to treat the effects of the virus? Is that why they don't work the way anyone expected on me?" Linc had mentioned something about Thavasi being more like puppy love in her case. It sounded as if that wasn't a common reaction. "How can you market a drug that won't work for everyone, and why one that changes your emotions so much?"

Dr. Turtle sat down in the chair next to her and started typing. The security screens went black one by one.

Alice kept talking. "No one knows for sure why the virus didn't affect me." *Or so everyone but Dr. Turtle thinks.*

Gryff mumbled, "There isn't a trace of it in your system."

There wouldn't be. On the first day she tested positive for WonderLand, Dr. Turtle had told her that he'd changed the results because it wasn't safe for her. If she told anyone, she'd be putting their lives at risk. He would continue to treat her, but they would never mention her infected status again, not even to ask her about the side effects.

So, she'd kept the secret, even from Kaleb. It was the only thing she'd kept from him, and she'd gotten pretty good at it.

How do I get the information I need without alerting Gryff to the fact that I've been infected this entire time?

Alice studied the doctor, and an idea came to her. "After all the blood, saliva, and tests over the past two years, there's still no sign?" she asked.

"W-well," Dr. Turtle stuttered. "That's not exactly true."

"Alex," Gryff snapped. "It's not a good idea."

Dr. Turtle looked up at Gryff. "She has a right to know." He sat up straighter and met Gryff's eyes. "I'm going to tell her." Dr. Turtle turned to her. "Th-that is, if you want to know. It's not a happy story."

Alice's plan had worked. *Look like you know what's going on, and they will fill in the blanks.* She nodded, indicating Dr. Turtle should continue.

"Let's start with the tests we've done on you. It's true we can't find the exact reason why WonderLand didn't affect you like the others, or why it isn't now." He looked back at Gryff and then turned back to Alice, sharing a look with her that indicated that Dr. Turtle hadn't told Gryff she had the virus. "It causes a violent insanity in most people, and in others, a childlike euphoria."

That explains the security guards.

"Although." He tapped his fingers on the metal table. "Now that I think about it, I've only seen the euphoria once, a few months before the theater."

"Wait, what?" Alice was confused about how they could know so much about a virus that had been released three times. Only the theater had taken place long enough ago to study and she was the only survivor.

Dr. Turtle pulled on his collar. "This is the part... Well, Gryff, play the video."

Gryff's long arm stretched across the table and pressed enter on the keyboard in front of him, a scowl on his face. "I hope you know what you're doing," he muttered.

The wall of monitors lit up, and a theater full of people watching a movie filled the screens. Pink smoke rolled in through the doors, down the stairs, and over the people. Alice looked away from the center of the screen to the yellow numbers in the right corner; it was dated two years before her mother's death.

Alice met Dr. Turtle's probing gaze.

"We ran fifteen tests before yours, and each time participants were docile or childlike," Gryff said.

Tests?

Alice watched the people in the theater. Some danced like ballerinas or oohed and aahed at the colors changing on the screen.

Gryff pressed a button, and the date changed. "We hadn't noticed at first." He pointed to a guy in the middle row. "There were a few people who weren't affected."

Dr. Turtle mumbled, "There are always a few weirdos in a crowd."

Gryff continued. "Once we realized it, Reid had to find out why. The people working on WonderLand started to add things, things that have been known to cause hallucinations." Gryff shook his head. "That's when your mother came to me with her concerns. I referred her to the Task Force. They had been investigating Red Queen Inc. for human rights violations.

"Everything was going fine. She was collecting evidence. She even found a way to switch out some of the worst versions for a weaker one—that is, until the day of her death."

The yellow date stamp on the right corner of the screen changed to the date of the tragedy. Alice tried to look away, anywhere but at the center of the screen, but it didn't work. She needed to know what happened that day.

The screen was frozen on a set of double doors. The doors had a thick metal chain running through the handles, trapping the occupants inside.

"Your mother thought it was a celebration of the progress of her work, on finding a...well, it's not important. She wouldn't have brought you if she knew it was going to be one of the Queen's experiments."

A teenage boy walked in front of the screen. The way his boots scraped the floor reminded Alice of someone, but she couldn't place him. His black gloves clasped a small shiny box. It was a heavy-looking lock. He pulled the lock through the chains, blocking the door. Then he spoke into a walkie-talkie he'd pulled from his waist. Alice moved closer to the screen. Blond curls stuck out from under a black hat. *It couldn't be. He would never.* The boy turned to face the screen, and it was Kaleb, her Kaleb, glaring at the camera.

Her insides went cold, and Gryff's voice turned to static. *If those doors hadn't been blocked off, there would have been more survivors.*

Alice closed her eyes and turned away from the screen. She didn't need to see any more. "Turn it off."

A loud knock sounded at the door.

Dr. Turtle changed the monitor back to the inner workings of Red Queen. The camera showed Kaleb, his blond hair bright against the gray of the hallway outside, his hand raised to knock a second time.

Alice's vision flickered.

Chapter 20

Alice watched Gryff and Kaleb as they moved the desk back, blocking the door, again. Her vision flickered between color and black and white. Alice clenched her fists at her side, holding onto reality with whispered numbers on her lips. *He was there.* She tried not to glare at Kaleb as he and Gryff started back toward her. She had told Kaleb almost everything about that day, about trying to hide, about being dragged by her hair, and about her mother. She had watched her mother die as she protected Alice from the rest of the Infected. He'd known and said nothing.

Kaleb had a slight limp, and sweat dripped from his blond hair. Their eyes met, and a wide smile spread across his mouth. For a second, his eyes sparkled with relief or maybe affection, but then that spark disappeared.

He took a tentative step forward. "Ace?"

The colors of the world drained from Alice's vision. All she saw was the boy who had stolen her heart and then betrayed her. She raised her hand, nails out, ready to tear his skin away from the bone. She imagined the warm blood from his open wounds on her fingertips and his pain-filled screams. She imagined the thrill of not having to hold on to her control. She would finally be free. *No more hiding my true feelings from the world.*

I won't let him win.

Wait... No. I...I'm fine. I'm fine, echoed through her mind.

Those two words had kept her from going mad in the theater and every day since. Color seeped back into the room, starting at the edges, slithering its way into the center.

Alice met Kaleb's concerned eyes, then she raised her hand and slapped him. She did it not because of the virus, but because he betrayed her, pretending to be...whatever they were to each other.

Kaleb rubbed his cheek, a red handprint under his fingers. "What was that?" He looked behind her. "Shit."

Alice turned her back on him and noticed someone had put the video of him locking the theater doors on the screen again.

She turned back around. "You were there." She stood up straight, her shoulders back. "You locked them, us, in. Someone other than me could have survived if you hadn't."

He stepped closer to her. "I know."

"You know." Alice hit Kaleb's chest. "No 'sorry, I didn't want to do it'?" She hit him again, and this time he stumbled backward. "How about 'you don't understand.'"

Kaleb looked down at the ground for a moment before looking at Alice. She met his gaze. He'd put up a wall, but Alice didn't care. He had lied to her.

She pushed him. "How about the classic 'I was going to tell you'? Or whatever else people say when they screw up and don't want it to be their fault."

"Would it change anything?" he asked. "I hate myself for what I did and even more that I've kept it from you." Kaleb reached for her.

Alice stepped back. She wanted to run, to be anywhere but here. She'd come into this hellhole to save him, and he'd betrayed her.

"We have to go," Kaleb said.

A tear rolled down Alice's cheek. She whispered, "Why would I go anywhere with you?"

"Alice, since that day I've done everything in my power to protect you. I'm doing the same now." Kaleb closed the gap between them, using his thumb to wipe the tear off her cheek, leaving a red spot on his finger.

Her throat ached. She knew what that bloody tear represented. She had almost lost control, become like the others under the virus's influence. Kaleb may have lied to her about being there, and at some point, they'd have to deal with that, but right now she needed to calm down.

Alice moved away from Kaleb but still stood close enough to study his face. She expected to see fear or anger in his eyes, but instead, he was the broken boy from when they first met. Alice's anger started to dissolve. His father had gotten him the job with Red Queen, and Alice was sure he'd forced his son to do the dirty work. It would explain Kaleb's hostility toward the man.

"I hope one day you will listen to my story."

Alice longed for the comfort of his touch and hated herself for it. He'd kept things from her. To be fair, she had done the same, although her secret hadn't caused anyone's death. Yet.

"I found a way out, kind of," Kaleb said.

"W-why 'k-kind of'?" Dr. Turtle stuttered.

Kaleb scanned the room, looking for something that wasn't there. His expression changed to one of defeat, and Alice knew he wasn't sure what to do. Kaleb's forehead scrunched, his thoughts hidden. "Nothing has changed; we just have to leave now."

"But." Gryff cleared his throat.

Dr. Turtle stuttered, "What about the Infected?"

Kaleb met her eyes. "We'll have to chance it."

Can I trust him? Does it matter? I want out of this building, and away from anyone that had anything to do with WonderLand or Red Queen. Right now, that means playing along.

"Then let's go," Alice said.

Chapter 21

Kaleb held out his hand for the gun he left with Alice. She handed it over without looking at him. Her cheek was still stained with the red tear he'd wiped away.

Alice is losing control, and it's my fault. The secrets he'd kept to protect her were unraveling, like a tornado consuming his world.

With Gryff's help, he opened the door and stopped the group in the doorway. He told them it was to check the hallway for any threats, but he needed to check the phone, make sure they were going the right way.

Kaleb typed in the password, and a map of the building came up on the screen, a red dot marking their location. White lines acted as a guide to the extraction point. The cold steel of Gryff's gun pushed into Kaleb's spine. "You better not be leading us into a trap."

Kaleb shoved the phone into his front pocket, cursing himself for being so careless. If Gryff saw what was on the phone... "This way."

They walked down the hall.

No one spoke, the only sound their footsteps. The gray walls of the hall were splattered with red blood every few steps. But no bodies. Kaleb hadn't noticed it before, but the only dead he'd seen had been Gryff's wife and the people in the office he'd hidden in earlier that day, and it had looked like they had succumbed to something other than the virus, maybe one of Turtle's drugs. It looked as if they had just given up. In all the WonderLand tests he'd witnessed as a teenager, no one had given up and died. They fought in some way. It had to be a drug.

Kaleb must have slowed down because Gryff's gun pushed further into his back, his hot breath near Kaleb's ear. "You forget where you're going, boy?"

The room in front of Kaleb blinked, the red on the wall changing to a dark, almost black, gray and then flashing back to the dark crimson of dried blood. Kaleb closed his eyes, picturing the map in his head.

"Next corner, turn right," he snapped.

Something was wrong, and he knew it. First the knife with Ryan, and now his vision was flashing between black and white and color. Sure, everything around him, besides the blood, was gray, but there was something else going on. The only explanation Kaleb could think of was the virus. Dr. Turtle had hinted at it being a possibility. If Kaleb was honest with himself, he wasn't one hundred percent certain how it was transmitted.

I always thought it was airborne. That was why smoke was used to disperse it. Kaleb looked down at his hand, remembering how the pink smoke of the virus had looked on his skin. *Could it be transmitted by touch?* He looked behind him. *Then why let Alice leave? No, that didn't make sense. Turtle said she had the virus since the theater.* Confused, Kaleb rubbed his head.

"Stop daydreaming." Gryff pushed him forward.

Kaleb heard not Gryff's voice but his father's, the man who tortured him for most of his childhood. He held the gun tight in his hand, feeling the grip cut into his skin. *Gryff was always a crazy son of a... If it weren't for Alice, I would...* Kaleb took a deep breath. *No. I'm not my father. I won't hurt Gryff, even if he is an asshole. Besides, we're almost to the exit. Then the Task Force can take Gryff and Dr. Turtle into custody—not that it will matter since the groups are working together. Maybe.*

He still wasn't sure about any of that, but it felt right.

Either way, it would give him and Alice a chance to slip away, go into hiding. No more double life. Be normal.

Of course, now that she had seen the tape, he would have to convince Alice to go with him. *Gryff showed that tape to her. He's trying to turn her against me.*

The hallway flashed between black and white and color.

Kaleb looked back at Alice again. She was talking to Dr. Turtle, not quite smiling at him, but she wasn't looking at him with disgust. *Even now, Turtle is convincing her not to be with me, making her hate me.* He stomped forward. *She doesn't care that I did it to protect her.*

Gryff pulled on Kaleb's shirt, slowing him down. Kaleb whirled around, ready to slug the jerk. The color drained from the world around him, changing to black and white. This time, the color didn't come back. Unable to explain away the sudden change, Kaleb's hand fell to his side. The only thing he could think of was that he was infected. There was no other explanation.

Gryff moved closer to Kaleb. "If you are leading me into a trap," he growled, looking back at Alice with an evil glint in his eye. "Well, what happened to your dear old mom will be nothing compared to what I do to your Alice."

Kaleb tried to take a deep breath to calm the anger that churned in his stomach, to remind himself he wasn't this person. The visions overwhelmed him. The gun. It glowed red in his hands. One shot could end this...quick.

Quick would be too easy, not what he wanted. Kaleb wanted Gryff to feel the same pain he had caused his mother and their family. Gryff had tortured her while Kaleb hid in the closet, listening.

The gun wouldn't be enough. He would need a knife. Kaleb could see it. The blade moving across Gryff's flesh, leaving a trail of crimson in its wake.

Of course, he would start with small, shallow paper-like cuts. The blood would rise to the surface in small streams and heal over almost as quickly as the cuts were made. Gryff would laugh at Kaleb's inability to torture someone, underestimating him, giving Gryff a false sense of victory. Then, and only then, would Rabbit push the blade deeper into his flesh, following the lines of the previous cuts, opening up the puckered scrapes, blood flooding over the open skin and coating the floor with its sticky metallic-smelling goo. His face losing its pink life tones, turning the greyish white color that accompanies death.

The flame of a torchlight would come to life and burn Gryff's flesh as Kaleb cauterized the wounds, stopping the life from seeping into a puddle on the floor. *That would be too easy.* Ice, he would use ice next. The thrill of the ways he could exact his revenge was like a live wire fighting to escape. *I would need at least a month to do it right.*

Kaleb knew the perfect place. He moved closer to Gryff, the gun in his hand still glowing red, the only color in the room.

"Everything okay?" Alice moved closer to them, the scent of her perfume overtook the violent visions.

Kaleb forced back the rage that wanted to take hold of him. *How does Alice live this way? Seeing the darkest part of yourself and not letting it take you over. How did she keep it a secret for so long?* It was taking everything in Kaleb to keep it together, to not let the violence that boiled inside him take over. Not wanting to make eye contact with Alice, afraid she'd see his secret, Kaleb looked down at his shoes. *I don't know if I can do this forever. I'm not as strong as her.*

"I'm fine," Kaleb growled.

She nodded, but her eyes moved up and down, looking him over. He still didn't meet her eyes, afraid she would see what he suspected. That he had lied to her, again.

Kaleb was infected, and he didn't think he could live with it.

Chapter 22

Alice watched Kaleb push through a set of double doors that opened with a pass of the phone, which shouldn't work, over a keypad. *There's something off about him; he's not acting quite right.* Kaleb motioned for their little group to follow. Alice expected it to be a hall like the others they'd walked through.

She took a step back, and a heaviness settled in her stomach as she scanned the large, brightly lit room lined with glass boxes. *There are people inside those boxes.* The occupants were in their late teens or early twenties and in different states of disarray.

They walked through the room, Kaleb and Gryff leading the way, Alice in back with Dr. Turtle. She watched the people in the boxes, trying to figure out why they were there, hoping this was where anyone who was exposed to the virus before the outbreak was placed. It was as good as any other explanation and the only thing she could think of since there was blood on some of the glass walls.

Black letters printed on the glass caught Alice's eye.

She stopped in front of one of the glass boxes; the word *Thavasi* was written in black on the glass above the air holes. *Thavasi was the drug Ryan used on me in the grocery store.* Alice swallowed, remembering how the drug had changed her emotions against her wishes.

A girl with dark eyes and hair stood behind the glass with red lipstick in her hand. Alice recognized her. Her name was Mary, and she was in one of Alice's classes. Alice hadn't seen her in months and assumed she'd dropped out and gone home. Mary had used red lipstick to draw on the glass little hearts with an A+M in the middle.

Alice wondered how Mary had gotten here and who A was and what A had done to Mary for her to hate him.

Dr. Turtle stood next to Alice. She could see the question in his eyes before he cleared his throat. He opened his mouth to ask, closed it, and turned to the glass to study the girl. They stood there for a few minutes listening to Gryff and Kaleb argue a few feet ahead.

"What is this place?" Alice asked.

"My lab, and these are my volunteers. Mostly college students. Don't worry, dear. They're perf-f-fectly safe. I locked down the lab when the alarm sounded."

"Alarms?"

He looked down at her, making her feel like a child. "Well, of course, dear, we do have safeguards. Can't have everyone infected by the things we're working on. We went over this the first time you came in."

She remembered they talked about safeguards, but nothing about alarms had been brought up. "Are the gas masks part of the safeguards?" she asked. "I saw a few people with them. They didn't seem to work, though."

"They wouldn't." Gryff walked past them and stopped near the last glass box. "WonderLand's not airborne, and those masks are decorations from one of the conference rooms," he grumbled.

That answers one question. "Why the smoke?"

Dr. Turtle walked toward Kaleb and Gryff, forcing Alice to follow. "Afraid that was Ms. Redding's idea. She has a bit of a flair for the dramatic. Something about primal fear and smoke. I didn't really listen when she explained her reasoning."

This didn't surprise Alice. The high heels she always wore gave her away—tall, bright, and full of personality.

They met Kaleb near a giant hole with two spinning fan blades. He typed something into his cell phone, and the blades started to slow down. "This leads to a network of tunnels that will get us out of Red Queen Inc." He turned to look at them. "Some ways are harder than others. I suggest staying to the left."

The blades stopped, and Gryff stepped into the opening. Alice stepped forward, but Dr. Turtle grabbed her wrist. "L-let." He took a deep breath. "Let me go first." She nodded, not sure why it mattered. He stepped through the hole, still holding Alice's wrist.

Alice placed her foot on the edge of the hole, ready to step through, when one of the large blades moved. She looked up at the sharp metal; it had moved maybe an inch, but Alice didn't want to be caught between the blades if they started again. She tried to move back, but Dr. Turtle still held Alice's wrist.

She tugged it toward herself and out of the way of the now-still blade. Dr. Turtle tightened his grip. Her pulse jumped in her throat. Images of the Infected and the theater hovered in the back of her mind.

"What are you doing?" Alice asked.

"Helping."

The fan's engine kicked on with a loud thump. Kaleb swore. Alice tried to yank her arm from Turtle's grasp. He pulled her closer. Alice looked up at the blade, her heartbeat drumming in her ear. The blade moved closer to her arm. "Let go," Alice screamed.

Turtle shook his head.

Where is Kaleb? Why isn't he helping?

Alice looked behind her, calling for Kaleb over the sound of the fan.

He didn't hear her; his eyes scanned the screen of his phone, probably trying to figure out why the fan's engine started again.

She called out to him again. He didn't move.

Alice swallowed the lump in her throat. She knew when Kaleb was too engrossed in what he was doing, when he closed out the world around him.

"Rabbit," she yelled, calling him by his nickname, which she never used, hoping he would find it odd enough to look up.

The blade moved a few inches, hovering over her bare skin. Sweat dripped down her brow. Alice pulled with all her strength, but she couldn't get away from the doctor, not alone.

Warm arms wrapped around her, pulling her away from the hole. *Finally.* Alice screamed out in pain, feeling the muscles in her shoulders separate. Kaleb whispered a few obscenities regarding Dr. Turtle in her ear before stepping away from her.

Alice watched the blade tick closer to her.

Kaleb yelled at Dr. Turtle, demanding he release Alice.

Turtle smiled at them and shook his head.

Kaleb moved behind Alice once again. "Together," he said.

She nodded, holding back nausea and fear.

"One," Kaleb said.

Coldness looped around Alice's wrist and moved down her back, settling there.

"Two," Alice said.

The blade ticked closer to her arm. Dr. Turtle removed one hand from Alice's wrist.

"Three."

They pulled together. Turtle released Alice moments before the fan started again, causing Alice and Kaleb to fall to the ground with a thump. They lay there for a minute catching their breath. Gryff's deep voice slashed through the buzz of the blades. "You'll have to find a different way out."

Kaleb grumbled low enough only Alice could hear. "Really, I hadn't noticed."

He stood looking past the blades of the fan. Gryff and Dr. Turtle had disappeared. Kaleb helped Alice to her feet, holding onto her arm. He traced the finger-shaped marks on her wrist. The lines of a glare etched on his face deepened with each sweep of his fingers.

She pulled her arm away from him. "It's fine."

"Yeah, you're always fine." He huffed before pulling out the phone.

It was a lie; Alice wasn't fine. She hadn't been in a long time. On top of all the crap she'd gone through, Kaleb had betrayed her, though every time he touched her or showed he cared for her made her forget that.

"I don't understand what happened," he grumbled.

Alice rubbed her bruised wrist, examining the bracelet that Turtle had slipped on her arm. Small plastic beads filled with multicolored liquid circled her wrist.

A tingling ran up Alice's spine.

Someone was watching her.

Alice looked over at Kaleb, but he had his head down, still looking at the phone. Besides, that wasn't the direction the eerie feeling of watching eyes came from.

She looked back at the fan, the blades spinning by. Dr. Turtle was staring at her from the other side. He placed his finger over his lips in a "shh" motion and then disappeared.

She had thought Dr. Turtle was trying to kill her as he held her arm captive, but now she wasn't sure. And he wanted her to keep the bracelet secret?

Alice watched Kaleb; he was staring at the damn phone.

"Now what?" she asked.

He slid the phone back into his pocket. "I guess we go out the way you came in."

Chapter 23

K aleb could feel himself slipping into the madness of the virus again. *I'm fine.* The color draining around him, Kaleb reached for Alice's hand, searching for an anchor. When their fingers met, color came back to his world, muted, but there. He let out a sigh of relief.

If he could hold on to his sanity long enough to get Alice out, it would be worth it. The underground entrance was designed to be an entrance only, nothing more, but if he could short out the door, maybe he could turn it into an exit.

Joseph's voice played in Kaleb's head, telling him he wasn't good enough. That he was worthless and stupid. His grip tightened on Alice's hand, causing her to pull back, but she didn't let go. He took a deep breath and loosened his grip. *Joseph isn't here. It's all in your mind.*

Kaleb needed a distraction, somewhere to direct his thoughts, a problem to solve. *If I could find out how the virus was released...* He didn't know what he'd do with the information, but it was a mystery that would need to be solved and would keep his mind focused on something other than his descent into madness.

"What were you and Dr. Turtle talking about earlier?" he asked.

"Nothing."

She was still mad at him. He could deal with that. "Did he tell you anything about how the virus got out?"

"Like what?"

Deep breath. "How it was released."

"No."

Okay, she wasn't going to help him. "Alice, I'm trying..." *To make peace. To apologize.* "You're being..." *Unreasonable.* "I only lied to protect you." *You have no idea what it's like. Not knowing who you can trust.*

He heard Alice's voice. "You could have trusted me. You chose not to. You chose to keep me in the dark, and without that knowledge, you endangered my life. But don't worry about it. I'm fine."

"You're always fine," Kaleb said.

Alice stopped. "What?" she asked.

Kaleb met her confused expression and realized she hadn't spoken, not since he asked her if she knew how the virus had been released. It had been in his head. He tried to shake away the effects of WonderLand.

"Nothing."

She stared at him for a few seconds. "Whatever."

Alice being angry with him was dangerous, even more so now that they were both infected.

Kaleb decided it might be best to be quiet and try to work out what had happened with the phone. Who had given it to Ryan? And who hacked it? *It was a safer topic. Less risk of having another imaginary conversation with Alice.*

At first, Kaleb thought the hacker might be Marci. It was possible. She wasn't in the building today, thankfully. Kit's ex showing up last night had forced Marci to go after her sister. Kaleb would take care of him later. *No, I won't. Get Alice out. Find Joseph. I can't leave Red Queen Inc. I'm infected and can't control it like Alice.*

Marci didn't have to be in the building to hack the phone, not if she was the one to program it, but why would she stop the fans? She wouldn't. It could have been DeeDee. Ryan said he got the phone from the Task Force.

But why would DeeDee do that?

It had to be DeeDee, though. A hacker working both sides, and not in the way he was. She didn't want to expose Red Queen. She wanted to keep their employees complacent. The bright girl he had bonded with over bubble gum and Red Vines had set him up. She lied to him, and if that wasn't bad enough, she had done it with his father, the man who had destroyed his life. It didn't matter that he had done things to protect Kaleb. He was a crappy father and an even worse person.

Who does that? Keeping a part of themselves hidden like that, protecting the people in their life. Kaleb realized he had done the same thing to Alice. *Me. That's who.* He looked down at their joined hands. It was why she was here, risking her life and her mind.

Kaleb thought of all the things he had kept from her and how they had led them to this moment. If he had only been honest with her, then she wouldn't be here. His vision flickered, and the room started to morph. Unlike last time when he'd imagined ways to kill Gryff, Kaleb was transported to a time he'd rather forget, drowning in feelings he'd buried deep.

Kaleb stared at himself in a mirror, the knife in one hand above his wrist and tears streaming down his face. He deserved this. They would be better off without him, he told himself. He knew it wasn't a rational thought, but he felt a truth to it. He pressed the blade into his skin. A trickle of red swirled into the white sink below.

Alice's voice broke through the vision. Her words surrounded him like static.

Kaleb stared into the mirror at his lifeless eyes, red from the tears. "This isn't real. I'm not here. I'm in Red Queen Inc., and Alice is in danger," he told his reflection. He hoped this place would disappear, but his reflection was still there. Laughing at him.

A warm hand wrapped around his wrist, and Alice's voice knocked around his skull. "Kaleb, stop."

Those two words pulled him back to reality.

He looked around. Somehow during his vision they'd made it to the security desk that the impromptu tea party had been earlier that day.

Three men stood with guns pointed at them. Pointed at Alice. One of them held Kaleb in place, the White Knight emblem on his right shoulder.

What have I done?

Kaleb couldn't remember how they got there, but he was sure he'd led them into a trap. He wasn't going to let them take Alice.

Kaleb aimed his gun at the leader, finger on the trigger.

Something smashed against his skull.

The world went dark.

CHAPTER 24

A lice raised her arms to surrender. *It's not like we could get out the way I came in anyway. It was only an entrance.* Once Alice had the cure, she was supposed to signal the Task Force to get her out. *That's not an option anymore either.* Kaleb had broken the glasses, her only means of communication with the Task Force, plus she still hadn't found the cure.

She'd tried to argue this point with Kaleb moments before. He hadn't listened, dragging her along behind him, muttering about how it wasn't safe to be here and that he needed to get her out. *Look where his need to be right has gotten us. Caught.*

"On your knees," the guard barked.

Alice obeyed.

Kaleb, on the other hand, stared down the man giving the orders. A scuffling of boots and bodies moved behind Alice. A crack sounded above her, and Kaleb crumpled to the floor next to her, unconscious.

One of the guards pulled Alice to her feet, dragging her through the building, the rubber on her shoes catching on the floor with every turn through the maze of halls.

A blue door with the number 323 printed in black swung open with a thud. The guard holding Alice led her into a large windowless room. A single fluorescent light humming with electricity illuminated the room. There were two cells with thick clear plastic bars and a rust-colored brick wall separating them. Each cell had a single bed and toilet in it. The guard pulled her toward the one on the right and shoved her in. The plastic bars vibrated when he slammed the cell shut.

Two men dragged Kaleb's limp body into the room. His face was marked with bruises and a small cut above his eyebrow. The cell door next to hers scraped open. She looked at one of the people holding Kaleb up. "Maybe you should leave him with me so I can tend to his wounds."

The guy looked toward the cell next to her and then back at her. They dragged Kaleb into the cell next to hers.

The mattress squeaked in protest with what she hoped was Kaleb being thrown on the bed. The door slammed shut, and the men shuffled past her, not saying a word before leaving her and Kaleb alone.

Alice listened for Kaleb's labored breaths, making sure he was still alive. *How had we gotten here?* A few weeks ago, they had been sitting in front of her computer watching a movie. Now they were trapped in cells in the middle of an outbreak surrounded by people who had lost their minds for no reason other than illness.

If that wasn't bad enough, she was still wrestling with whether or not it was a good idea to trust Kaleb. He had known about her mother and kept it from her. He'd befriended her most likely to see what she knew. Was all the stuff he told her about his dad true?

The springs of the twin mattress in the next cell squeaked, and Kaleb moaned. "Ace?"

"Perfect way to spend a Saturday night," she joked. When counting didn't work, Alice would try to use humor as a way to deal with anger, though it usually only worked with Kaleb.

Kaleb snorted and then wheezed. The guards who had brought them here must have slammed him pretty hard into the walls. "Not quite. We need Red Vines and a new Doctor Who episode."

She smiled, remembering the last Saturday night they'd spent together in her dorm room. They'd huddled around her little computer screen, the blue light shining on their faces. Of course, that was before she knew he was keeping secrets.

Wanting to be closer to him, she moved from her bed and slid down the wall that their cells shared.

Sitting on the floor, she asked the question that had been on her mind. "Kaleb, why did you keep your involvement with the day that my mother died from me?"

His sigh sounded close. Alice imagined he was sitting against the wall behind her, back to back, like they did when they spent long nights together studying.

The silence of the room was like a cold, lifeless blanket. She worried that he wouldn't tell her and was about to take back her question when he started to talk.

"Do you remember when you first met me?"

She nodded and then remembered he couldn't see her. "A fellow lost soul." Alice smiled at the memory.

She was in a hole-in-the-wall coffee shop, sipping lukewarm tea and staring at a blank screen, trying to figure out what to do with her life. A man walked into the shop, looking like a dark cloud ready to strike.

"You're in my seat," he grunted.

Alice looked him over, starting at the scuffed black boots and rumpled black jeans and ending with a Metallica T-shirt. He had long jet-black hair, the roots of his natural blond glowing like a beacon of his true self. His red-rimmed eyes stared down at her. They begged her to argue, make a scene, do something, and not treat him like nothing.

The red cushioned chair she sat in scraped the hardwood floor when she stood. The balding man at the next table over looked up from his newspaper and met Alice's gaze. He smiled back at her before adjusting his paper and ignoring the room again. She reached into her purse and pulled out bug-eyed fluorescent pink sunglasses and examined the chair. She looked first at the seat and then the back, and she even got on her knees to look underneath.

"What are you doing?" Metallica T-shirt asked.

She pushed her short brown hair behind her ears and smiled at him. "I don't see it."

"See what?"

"I looked over every inch of this chair, and all I see is 'Alice' written in small black letters." She pushed the sunglasses up to rest on her head.

A smile touched the edge of his red lips. "Alice, huh. I don't see it."

"Oh, I forgot, you'll need these." She handed him the bright pink sunglasses and in a stage whisper said, "Invisible ink."

He took the glasses from her with a chuckle. The smile he'd been trying to hide spread across his face, lighting his features. The fluorescent pink of the sunglasses shone in the sea of black that was his look. "Look here, between 'Alice' and 'Alice was here.'" He ran his finger across the back of the red leather and stopped in the center of the cushion. "'Rabbit.'"

"Rabbit?"

He slid the glasses down his nose, his blond eyebrow lifted. "Nicknames. You don't get to pick them, just have to live with them."

"Tell me about it," she mumbled.

Alice shook herself from the memory. "What does that have to do with anything?"

The sound of Kaleb's boots scraping against the concrete floor echoed in the empty room. "I'd be lying if I told you I hadn't recognized you that day. Maybe that was why I approached you. I thought if you were okay, then maybe I could... I don't know. Then you made me laugh. It was the first time I had smiled in months."

"Me too," she admitted.

"It was a good day, and I was going to leave it at that, a chance meeting. Even if I wanted to spend more time with you, it wouldn't be fair to you. I couldn't tell you about my involvement with Red Queen and that day. I knew keeping it a secret would destroy whatever we became. DeeDee saw me talking to you, and she came to me. We'd worked together for Red Queen Inc., me because of my father and her because of her sister." He sighed. "Anyway, after what happened at the theater, she joined the Task Force. It was set up to take down Red Queen Inc. and everyone involved with WonderLand."

He cleared his throat. "They needed someone to get close to you, to find out how much you knew and why Redding had taken an interest in you. The Task Force approached DeeDee at first. She was supposed to try and befriend you, but DeeDee knew you would never let her get close to you, not after the theater."

"She was right."

She'd told herself every time DeeDee came around it wasn't her fault what happened in the theater, but Alice couldn't get past the fact that DeeDee was there that day. She'd left moments before the chaos without a real explanation.

Kaleb didn't say anything about Alice's admission, but she imagined a sad smile crossed his lips before he went on with his story.

"DeeDee reminded me of the terrible things her sister had done, not only to perfect strangers but to one she claimed to care about. She told me you could become one of her victims again. After that meeting, I knew I would do anything to keep you safe."

Alice didn't know what to say or how to deal with what he told her. She concentrated on trying to understand why there was so much interest in her. She'd been infected, but only Dr. Turtle knew that. Alice turned the bracelet Dr. Turtle had given her around her wrist, letting the cool fluid-filled beads soothe the bruise.

She cleared her throat. "I wasn't the only one unaffected by the virus, was I?"

"No, but you are the only one Redding took an interest in, that anyone took an interest in." He exhaled. "Alice, I saw everything that happened that day. It was different than any of the other experiments."

She heard his feet shuffling across the concrete and assumed he had started to pace. He only did that when he was trying to figure something out.

"I sat there, safe behind a computer screen, knowing it was

happening but too scared to do anything. When it was all over, I looked around the room, and the only person who shared in my horror was DeeDee. Redding was smiling as if she had hoped for that very thing to happen. That is, until they found you." The shuffling stopped. "I don't know what she wants with you, but I couldn't let anything happen to you again."

"Is that why you came up with the plan to run?"

"They wanted me to bring you in."

"Did you drug me?" She thought it was Ryan, but she needed to hear it from him.

"That was Ryan, but I was supposed to. I was told to make it look like you had lost your mind, had a delayed reaction to the virus. Not Redding's first plan, or a really good one at that. But then, as far as she knew, you never made it to the lake."

Alice gasped. "Wait, the lake—that was on purpose?"

"The water was laced with the newest version."

All this, just so Redding could get her hands on me. "Why wouldn't she do it while I was here for my weekly appointment?" she asked.

"I don't know."

Alice thought for a moment before asking, "Why not take me into the Task Force?"

The bed squeaked again, but he didn't answer her question.

The overhead lights turned on, giving the room a yellow glow, and the door in the far right corner rattled. She heard Kaleb trying to stand in the cell next to her, and she did the same. Two people entered the room. It was Madison and Harrison in their rumpled black uniforms, but something was off about them, even more so than the last time she'd seen them.

"What's going on?" she asked Madison.

Harrison grinned. "A trial."

Madison elbowed him. "No talking to the prisoners."

"Oh, right."

The two men turned their backs toward the bars.

"Whose trial?" Alice asked.

"That is a secret," one of them called out.

Alice looked at the two men, wondering what had happened to them since she'd last seen them. It had only been a few hours since Madison made her a paper hat and Harrison gave her coffee in a lipstick-stained cup.

Harrison stepped in front of Kaleb's cell with a key that matched the bars. They pulled Kaleb from the cell, his hands trapped by metal handcuffs in front of him.

"Where are you taking me?" Kaleb demanded.

They dragged him to the door, answering his question in unison as the door closed behind them. "Your father sent us."

Chapter 25

Madison removed the handcuffs from Kaleb's wrists before pushing him into the same room that he'd found Ryan in earlier that day, into the same bloodstained chair that Ryan had occupied an hour before. He knew he shouldn't have left Alice alone, but if anyone could help him get her out, it would be his father. Of course, it would cost him. Whatever the price was, it would be worth it if it meant saving Alice.

Kaleb stared at the floor, images of the things that could have caused the stains flashing through his virus-muddled mind. Excitement ran through him as WonderLand stirred in his veins, reminding him of his mistrust of Ryan. *The things I could do to Ryan...*

He heard his father's deep voice, and that rage started to build, changing those visions to the things he could do to hurt Joseph.

Rough hands forced Kaleb further into the chair.

He fought against them, but he wasn't strong enough to get away. It wasn't long before the cold steel of metal handcuffs wrapped around his arms again. For the third time that day, he was attached to a chair. *At least this time it's not a rolling chair,* Kaleb thought as he watched the guards walk out the door.

They left the door open a crack. Joseph's voice drifted into the room. "I don't care. Find it," he snapped. "My son is not leaving this room without it."

Find what?

Someone outside stammered, "But the Queen wants—"

"I don't care about the Queen," Joseph growled. "Find it."

Joseph came into the room, slamming the door shut on Tom's scared face. He turned to focus on Kaleb.

Kaleb was sure a dark bruise was forming on his cheek. He waited for his father to say something about it. He even had a smart remark ready, but Joseph didn't say anything. Instead, he turned around and opened the door, firing one shot into the hall. "I said to bring him to me uninjured."

He slammed the door shut, muffling the wails of whoever he'd shot. Kaleb wasn't sure if Joseph was infected, but his mind focused on the idea of it. *How long before I'm as far gone as Joseph? A monster with no regard for life.*

Joseph walked across the room, the gun still in his hand. Kaleb tightened his grip on the chair. *This may not have been my best idea.* This wasn't going to be one of their normal chats. No snarky comebacks. This was one of his father's fact-finding meetings where the torture was going to be slow and painful. It was the only reason why Joseph would be upset about the bruises on Kaleb's face.

Kaleb closed his eyes, not wanting his father to see the hateful shimmer of the virus shining through. It was his one advantage. Once the effects of the virus took control, Kaleb would no longer feel the pain.

Suddenly the cold metal wrapped around his wrist fell away, hitting the floor with a clank. *Why would he take the handcuffs off?*

Kaleb opened his eyes, surprised to find Joseph kneeling in front of him, a small key in his hand, mumbling something about paranoid idiots. "Kaleb, I'm sor—" Joseph's phone, one of the few that worked in the building, rang. Kaleb looked down at the screen to see his older brother Markus's number lighting it. *Why would Markus call him? He hates him.* Joseph stood up and turned his back on Kaleb.

"What took you so long?" The muscles in Joseph's back tensed at whatever Markus said. "I don't want to hear excuses." A pause. "Then act like one." He started to pace in front of Kaleb. "You need to come get your little brother. I've sent you the coordinates."

Joseph hung up the phone and slid it into his back pocket, leaving Kaleb to wonder if maybe his father did care about him. As far as Kaleb knew, they hadn't spoken in five years, yet his father had reached out to Markus.

Running his hands through his hair, he turned back to Kaleb. Their eyes met, and Kaleb knew Joseph saw the infection swimming in his eyes. Kaleb had expected his father to be angry or fearful, but there was resolve.

"I can't leave," Kaleb said. "But Alice can."

Joseph opened his mouth to say something, stopping when the door opened. A short man in a brown suit stood in the doorway.

"The trial is starting," he announced.

"Everything will be fine." Joseph helped Kaleb to his feet. "Just play along."

Kaleb nodded. If it meant getting Alice out, he'd do whatever his father asked.

Chapter 26

Alice stared at the clock that hung on the wall above the door. It had been twenty minutes since the guard had taken Kaleb. The only reason she wasn't worried something horrible was happening was that they'd taken him to his father. She didn't understand their relationship; one minute Kaleb hated the man, and the next he was the only one that could save them, but Joe seemed to love his son.

The door below the clock slammed against the cinder block wall, knocking gray dust to the floor. A tall man stood silhouetted by bright fluorescent lights in the doorway. He walked toward Alice's cell, the sound of clinking keys echoing through the empty room. It wasn't until he stopped in front of her glass cage that she recognized Madison.

Alice opened her mouth to say something, but his eyes met hers, and she could see the shimmer in his gaze. Madison took a large key ring from his belt. He examined a round metal key and then the lock, looking at both twice before moving to the next one, which was smaller than the first and also metal. Alice looked down at the lock, wondering where he'd put the key since taking Kaleb away. The metal keys weren't going to work. She was going to tell him, but he already had the key in the lock, trying to force it to work.

A cracking noise from somewhere deep in the locking mechanism echoed through the room. *If the lock breaks, will I be stuck here forever?*

Madison yanked the key from the lock and threw the entire key ring against the wall behind him. "It's not here," he bellowed.

"I have it. I have the key," Harrison yelled as he barreled through the door, glancing at the keys on the floor as he passed them.

He'd made it only a few steps before he fell and dropped the key, causing it to slide across the gray floor toward the glass bars.

She reached out for it, her fingers brushing the jagged edge. *I almost have it.* She pressed her face against the glass bar, reaching out as far as her fingers would allow. Her hand moved across the cool floor before brushing across something warm and sticky.

Alice pulled back, looking toward where her hand had been. Madison had the key clasped in his meaty fists. *Is he running a fever?* Alice stood up, wiping what she was pretty sure was sweat from Madison on her jeans. Even if Alice hadn't seen the shimmer in his eyes, after touching his skin, she knew he was sick.

Madison stood up and aimed the key at the lock. Alice took a step away from the bars, trying to decide if it would be better to run or go with them. *They might be taking me to Kaleb. Or my death.* Madison missed the keyhole, and the scraping sound of glass on glass moved across Alice's skin.

A vein pulsed in Madison's neck. He mumbled something under his breath to do with tea. This time he got a bit closer to the lock, but the scraping of glass on glass lasted longer.

Madison kicked the bars, causing dust to sprinkle on the ground in front of him. Red blood started to stream down his cheeks. He was losing control.

Alice moved to the furthest corner of the cell and looked for something she could use to knock him out. Madison wiped the blood tears from his face and onto his dark pants. She let her vision flicker, looking for the telltale sign of crimson lighting some kind of weapon. *Nothing.* The only thing in the room was a small bed and a toilet.

The key scraped across the lock again. Another miss.

Think, Alice, there has to be something you can do.

Her hands brushed against the pockets of her jeans. She'd forgotten about the key to Kaleb's car. Alice gripped it tightly in her right hand, prepared to battle. She wouldn't be able to get through to Madison this time. He was too far gone to help her.

The lock clicked.

Madison pushed open the cell door. It slammed into the brick wall, causing more dust to litter the floor. Alice sank back into the corner, the key between her fingers, ready to fight.

Harrison came up behind Madison. He placed a hand on his arm and whispered something in his ear. Alice thought about ducking between the two men and running for the door. She took a few steps forward, looking for an opening, but Harrison moved in front of her, blocking the way. He held a hand out to Alice. She looked into his steel-colored eyes. They didn't hold the shimmer that Alice associated with the virus. There was something else there, though. Something wasn't quite right, but it wasn't WonderLand.

Madison moved closer to them, his heavy breathing reminding Alice of the worst day of her life and the guy with the dark glasses. She started to count, telling herself that it was a long time ago. *This isn't the same.*

Alice noticed that blood was smeared on his hands and hoped it was from his eyes and not someone in Red Queen Inc.

"Time to go. The trial has started, and we're late," Harrison said.

"Trial?" She swallowed. "Whose?" She hoped it wasn't Kaleb's.

He looked back at Madison, and some sort of unspoken conversation passed between them. "I'm not sure," Harrison said and clasped Alice's arm.

He led her out of the cell and through the open door.

"Just follow the Queen's orders, and everything should be fine." Madison grabbed her other arm tight, his jaw ticking with forced control.

"Hopefully," Harrison mumbled.

Alice let them lead her down the hall, working to keep her fear under control while trying to memorize the winding hallways.

She tried to ignore the two security guards who chatted about coffee and cupcakes like nothing had changed. She stole a glance at Madison's eyes. Blood no longer dripped down his face, and the shimmer had faded. The conversation seemed to calm him and the effects of the virus. Maybe he wasn't too far gone. Maybe she could save him.

That is, if she ever found the cure; it was the only reason she'd come to this place. Well, that, and to save Kaleb, even if his loyalties didn't lie with her.

They stopped in front of a set of doors she had never seen before.

Harrison took a deep breath before pushing her through them. Alice stumbled into the room, almost falling face-first into a group of people who sat in red plastic chairs.

She straightened, studying the room. It was set up as a courtroom, and Alice had been pushed into the general assembly section.

At the front of the room, twelve people in gas masks and lab coats sat at two long skinny tables that faced a red cushioned chair that looked out of place in an office building. *It would fit better in a beauty pageant.* Alice studied the chair, fascinated by its presence and distracted by it. Either way, it kept her from the madness around her.

The chair was at the front of the room on top of a dark red platform, looming above the audience. She walked further in, closer to the chair. *It's a throne.* A velvet cushion covered the dark oak chair decorated with gold-etched leaves. No, not leaves. She squinted to get a better look. There were drops of... Was that blood? Whatever it was, it started at the top center of the chair.

Disgust mixed with a bit of fear in her throat. Alice followed the drops with her eyes, focusing on the top of the throne. In the center, a heart split into two halves. *Who would sit in that?*

Joseph walked across the front of the room, Reid following close behind. She stopped in front of the throne and glared at the crowd. They ignored her.

She leaned down, whispered something into Joe's ear, shrugged, and then plopped into the throne. Sliding the crimson pumps that matched her business suit under the throne, Reid moved her bare feet under her, curled into a ball, and closed her eyes.

If Alice had any doubts about Reid being on something, at that moment they disappeared. Reid was always put together and professional, insisting on being referred to as Ms. Redding by everyone, except for her sister and Alice. The woman Alice knew would never take her shoes off in public, and sleeping in public was out of the question.

Joe stood next to the throne, guarding Reid. Until this moment, she hadn't realized how much Kaleb and his father looked alike, with the same build and intense gaze. The only difference was the hair color; Kaleb's was sandy blond, but his dad was a salt-and-pepper black.

The Queen woke long enough to bellow, "Bring in the accused."

Kaleb walked through the doors at the front of the room by himself, unrestrained. He was covered in even more bruises, and blood trickled from his lip. Alice took a step forward, but Madison pushed her into a nearby chair. She tumbled onto the person sitting in the next chair over. "Hey," Tom whispered angrily.

"Sorry," she said. "I was pushed."

"That's no excuse," he huffed.

Alice wanted to tell him "of course it was," but she bit back her comment, feeling it was best to keep her mouth shut. She wasn't sure what he would do if he recognized her. Instead, she turned in her chair so he couldn't see her face but she could still see what was going on in front of the room. It didn't matter though. Tom fell asleep and began snoring lightly next to her.

Kaleb dragged a chair across the carpeted floor and placed it next to Reid's throne. Joe came back into the room dragging a tall man whose hands were cuffed together in front of him. Joe shoved him into the chair Kaleb had placed next to Reid's throne a moment before. The man kept his eyes focused on the floor, not looking into the crowd. The room broke out in whispered conversations.

"Who do you think it is?" the woman in front of Alice asked.

"No, he died," someone a few rows behind said.

"What about?" a woman in front started.

"Fired," Tom sleepily mumbled next to her.

Alice knew who it was sitting in that chair. She didn't need to see his face to know; for one horrible afternoon she had been completely in love with him. There was something about caring about someone, even if it was drug induced, that made them unforgettable.

His name escaped her lips. "Ryan."

The stocky woman in front of Alice turned to look at her and then tapped the person next to her. "She knows the accused."

People around the room turned to look at Alice and whispered about her. Even Tom had woken up from his nap to stare.

Alice sank into her chair, trying to disappear.

A loud whistle sounded at the front of the room, and the Queen's voice called out. "I will have order in this court."

The room went silent as she glared at the crowd before throwing a shoe at Joe.

"Rabbit, read the charges," Joe barked.

A woman in the crowd yelled, "Off with his head."

"Here, here," said a male voice.

The rest of the crowd clapped and nodded in agreement. A few people even hooted. Alice swallowed the bile that had risen to her throat. *They're going to kill him.* Ryan had done some horrible things —a lot of them to her—but he didn't deserve to die.

"Silence." The Queen glared at the crowd and tapped her fingers on the arm of the chair before she stepped down from her throne.

Alice watched Reid slide her bare feet across the floor like an ice skater, stopping in front of Ryan. It was the only time Alice had seen her without high heels, and it felt wrong.

"Look at me," she demanded.

Ryan's gaze didn't change.

Reid grabbed his chin and forced him to meet her eyes. Alice looked for the shimmer of the virus. Anger radiated from him, but his eyes were clear.

Ryan spat, missing Reid by inches. The crowd gasped and then fell into complete silence, waiting to see what Reid would do next.

"Where are my tarts?" she said through gritted teeth.

Tarts?

Ryan smiled, his once bright white teeth stained red. "You will never find them."

The Queen slapped him, the sound echoing through the near silence of the room. His smile widened, and she raised her hand to hit him again. Joe stepped between them and seized Reid's wrist in one firm hand. Something passed between them, and the Queen's shoulders seemed to relax, but she still glared at Joe before stomping back to her chair.

Joe nodded to Reid before speaking to Ryan. "I have only two questions, and then you will be free to leave."

"I won't tell you where they are."

Kaleb's dad turned to the crowd. "We have already located them," he said. The right side of Joe's lip came up with a half smile. Alice knew he was lying. He had the same tell as his son. She had noticed Kaleb's tell when they played card games.

"Did you poison the Queen and her people?" Joe asked.

By poison, does Joe mean infect? Alice looked around the room. *How many of them have WonderLand running through their veins? How long before the room breaks out in violence?*

Ryan was silent.

"We've seen the tapes of you in the lab."

Had he released the virus in Red Queen Inc., or were the tapes from when he took the Thavasi? If Ryan had released the virus, then why come back? It had to have been from when he stole the Thavasi. Besides he would've been in Task Force custody at the time of WonderLand's release.

"You deserve to die horrible, painful deaths." Ryan looked around the room. "For the unlawful experiments, kidnappings, killings."

Kaleb moved so fast across the room, Alice was surprised, but she was even more surprised when he punched Ryan in the stomach. Something that looked like a conversation passed between the men before Reid spoke, a broad smile spread across her lipstick-stained lips. "Why come back?"

Ryan lifted his cuffed hands and pointed. "Because of her. Because of Alice Smith."

Chapter 27

The room exploded into chaos, everyone speaking at once, pointing and staring at Alice. She barely noticed, though.

Why would Ryan come back here for me? He doesn't even know me.

She looked around the room at the people near her. Their eyes bored into her, and a few of the voices broke through.

"She's not Alice."

"Looks just like her mother."

The whistle sounded again, and silence ruled the room.

Joe's voice boomed at the front. "Our next witness, Alice Smith." He looked at Alice. "Please step forward."

Kaleb's fear-filled eyes met hers. Faking confidence she didn't feel, Alice stood and tried to give Kaleb a reassuring smile. *This is bad. No one was supposed to know who I am.*

Pushing her shoulders back and holding her head high, Alice walked down the aisle to the front of the room. She let the whispered conversations drift past her the same way she did in high school. If only she could do the same with the butterflies in her stomach.

Madison and Harrison dragged Ryan off to the next room. Alice looked over at the jurors and noticed they were all asleep. She wanted to say something, but a loud bang like a gunshot came from the room where Ryan had been dragged.

Alice gulped down a scream and kept her eyes focused on the courtroom. *Freedom meant death. Had anyone even noticed the gunshot, or did they not care?*

She looked around the room. Joe, his jaw clenched and shoulders tight, held back the anger that was radiating from him. In contrast was Reid, who was dozing on her throne, her slack face reminding Alice of DeeDee and her mission with the Task Force.

Even if I escape the trial and find the cure, there's no way out. Kaleb had destroyed her only way to communicate with the Task Force and her exit plan. Now what? Alice realized she would not be leaving this place alive, but instead of fear, she felt free. Free to say whatever she wanted.

Joe approached her, his blue eyes staring down at her. The light caught the shimmer of virus that swam in their depths, reminding Alice he was infected. *Had he been before?*

Joe handed her a piece of crumpled white paper. "Read this," he demanded.

Alice flattened the paper the best she could before looking at the crisp black wingdings printed on the page. *This has to be a joke.* She looked up at Joe, who had a goofy smile on his face, and back down at the paper. Kaleb's breath brushed against the back of her neck, and she knew he was looking at the piece of paper in her hand.

He read out loud. "Airplane, smiley face, cross, telephone." He met Alice's eyes, and she could see the confusion on his face. "A bull?"

Waking up from her slumber, Reid said, "That is the most important evidence we have heard."

The crowd murmured their agreement; some even wrote it down in little black notebooks. One was typing it onto some kind of tablet, or at least he was trying to. Alice could see there was no light coming from the screen.

Alice whispered to Kaleb, "This is ridiculous."

"Speak up," the Queen yelled.

Kaleb clasped Alice's shoulder in warning. She wasn't going to repeat what she said, but for some reason, she was tempted to throw a temper tantrum. "I said that it doesn't make any sense."

"Of course it does," Joe scoffed.

Feeling the weight of Kaleb's fear on her shoulder, Alice tried to shrug off his hand, without success. "Then explain it," she said.

Kaleb's strained whispered voice met her ear. "What are you doing?"

She wasn't sure. Why would she have this hostile attitude with a room full of people who not only were losing their minds but were also armed with sharpened letter openers, chopsticks, and other items found in an office building. One guy had a red in-case-of-fire ax duct-taped to his thigh.

"Well, that's easy," Joe started. "Of course the airplane is referring to Delta, which is one of the letters in the sorority you belong to, correct?"

Alice nodded, not sure where he was going with this.

"The sorority makes you happy, hence the smiley face. The cross is evident. You are at a crossroads." He looked at the crowd. "The telephone—you need to call someone."

The crowd oohed and aahed while Alice rolled her eyes. "What about the bull?"

"Well, you must be a Taurus," Reid said.

She wasn't.

Joe smiled at her. "Of course, that's it."

"So you think this has to do with astrology," Alice scoffed. "It's gibberish."

She stood up and faced Reid. Her clear eyes met Alice's, a glint of surprise shining in them. *Reid isn't infected. I saw the infection there, hadn't I?* Now she wasn't sure. This was the real Reid, a psycho, surrounded by her court of bloodthirsty killers. *How did I not see it before?*

Reid smiled at her before turning to the court. "Off with her head."

Chapter 28

Alice couldn't move, fear freezing her in place. Images of the theater mixed with the things she had seen today. *I should have died that day.*

Kaleb grabbed her arm in a tight grip and dragged her toward the room where Madison and Harrison had shot Ryan.

She watched the people in the room move toward them and knew she needed to run, but she was stuck somewhere between the past and the now.

The violence of the virus finally took over the room. One of the women, the one who'd said Alice looked like her mother, had a sharpened chopstick raised above her head, ready to jam it into the throat of the guy with the ax.

Kaleb pushed through the door at a sprint, pulling Alice with him. She'd expected to see Ryan's cold dead eyes looking up at her, but he wasn't there. The room was empty; there was no blood on the white walls or floor, no sign of what happened.

Kaleb tightened his grip on Alice's hand, reminding her Reid and Joe and quite possibly the rest of the courtroom weren't far behind.

She stumbled forward, tripping over her feet.

"Almost there," Kaleb panted.

They moved through the double doors that led into the lobby and ran past the security desk and the mismatched tables, still covered with an assortment of cups and paper hats. *We're going back the way I came in.*

Kaleb slammed the door open, pushing Alice through. The closet-sized room hadn't changed; the lab coats and security uniforms still lined the walls, and the mirror door was still sealed closed.

She asked through labored breaths, "What now?"

"I get you out of here." He took a step toward the mirror.

"How?"

Someone told her this was a one-way door. Kaleb tapped a card against the mirror, a reflection of his smiling face and dyed hair looking back at them. After a few seconds, a small box with four colored squares appeared in the mirror above his ID. Black block letters moved across the top of the glass. **Good evening, Rabbit. How can I help you today?**

"You knew how to get out this way the entire time?" she fumed.

"Yes. No. I wasn't sure if this would work. It shouldn't during a lockdown." He tapped on the squares, and a tune Alice couldn't place came from the keypad. Each tap of a square sounded its own tone.

"You could have told me," Alice said.

Something hard slammed against the door behind them, causing the hinges to squeak.

"This isn't really the time to argue." Kaleb tapped a few more keys, and red dust from outside blew across their feet.

The room shook with the next slam against the door. Alice looked back at it; the wood was splintered. "You're right," she agreed.

The mirror slid up partway, revealing the dark room and ladder Alice had used to get into Red Queen earlier that day. *Had it only been a few hours?* She reached down to take Kaleb's hand.

The door behind them cracked, and they both turned around. A hairy arm reached through a hole looking for the doorknob.

"Time to go." Kaleb pushed Alice through the opening left by the raised mirror.

The door behind them opened, and Madison rushed in, blood

flowing from his eyes.

"Go," Kaleb yelled.

Alice clasped Kaleb's arm, trying to pull him through the opening with her. She wasn't going to leave him here. Kaleb didn't budge. She pulled on him, begging him to move.

He shook his head. "I can't."

Kaleb looked into the light, and to her horror, Alice saw the shimmer of the virus filling his eyes. *How had I not noticed?* "It doesn't matter." She lived with the virus, and so could he. Alice pulled on his arm. "We'll figure it out together."

A sad smile crossed his lips. "I'm sorry, but I'm not as strong as you." He pushed Alice through the opening, hard enough that she not only cleared the door but fell against the metal rungs of the ladder, knocking the wind out of her.

"Alice, *run.*"

Alice shook her head. She couldn't leave him to die.

Using the metal rungs, Alice pulled herself to a standing position, but her breath was still coming in short bursts, and she couldn't take more than a step or two before needing to stop.

The door started its slow descent. Kaleb watched her, silhouetted by the fluorescent lights behind him. A dark, hulking figure that Alice thought looked like Madison grabbed Kaleb around the waist and pulled him back.

She forced herself to move forward. *I won't leave him.*

Madison fell forward, huffing for air, and Kaleb took a step toward her. Alice reached out to him. Their fingers brushed. Warm arms wrapped around Alice's waist from behind. Someone pulled her away from Kaleb.

She kicked and screamed, trying to get away from her captor.

The door hovered, leaving enough room for Kaleb to escape.

"Kaleb," she called out.

He lay on the ground, red glinting off a gash on his forehead. His eyes met hers, and he mouthed the words "I'm sorry."

The door slammed shut, plunging the room into darkness.

Chapter 29

The vice-like grip that held Alice in place fell away, and she ran to the keypad next to the door. Her fingers pressed the keys that should have opened it, but nothing happened. No snarky comments from the computer. No colors flashing across the keypad. Just a bright white **ERROR**.

Alice screamed and slammed her fist against the closed door. "You don't get to do this."

A light turned on behind her.

She spun around, ready to fight off her captor. The yellowish light of a lantern lit up the sharp features of his face, and even though she'd only seen him a handful of times, Alice recognized Kaleb's brother Markus.

"Alice." He took an uneasy step toward her, his voice low as if talking to a wounded animal. "We have to go."

"Go... But Kaleb. We can't go."

Markus moved closer. "Kaleb sent me to get you."

Alice stared at him, confused. *When had Kaleb contacted him? Why had Kaleb sent him? But he'd let Kaleb be captured.*

"I..." She didn't know what to say.

Kaleb is infected.

Alice's legs gave out. She slid down the wall, the cold of the steel door seeping through her shirt. She didn't know what to do.

Markus sat down next to her, kicking up dirt as he moved. He didn't say anything.

She stared at the powder as it settled into place, her mind blank. She needed to do something. Sitting here was getting them nowhere, and Kaleb didn't have much time. That's when she saw the earpiece she'd lost.

The Task Force. They could help her get back in.

Alice grabbed the earpiece off the floor, wiped it across her jeans, and shoved it in her ear. She could hear Linc and DeeDee arguing on the other end and tried to get their attention, but they didn't hear her.

They had to be close.

With no way to respond, Alice stood and stomped across the room.

"Where are you going?" Markus called out to her.

"To save your brother." She clasped a rung of the ladder. "Are you coming?"

She didn't wait to see if he followed her but moved up the ladder, through the small room, and out into the early morning light. *Linc had mentioned they would have a truck in the Red Queen parking lot.* The problem was that it would take at least an hour to walk there. By then, it would be too late. She needed to find a faster way to get there.

Markus stumbled out the door behind her.

"Do you have a car?" Alice asked.

He pointed to a gray sedan parked close by. "What's the plan?"

"I need to talk to someone." She held her hand out. "Keys."

Markus didn't hesitate; he dropped the nondescript key into her hand. "Then?"

"We go back to Red Queen and get your brother."

Fearing Markus was going to try and talk her out of it, Alice got behind the wheel. Markus sat in the passenger seat without saying a word, his phone glued to his hand. Alice drove to the main entrance of Red Queen, thankful for the early hour and lack of other cars on the road; all the while Markus typed into his phone. Alice pulled the car behind the black van parked in front of the glass doors of Red

Queen headquarters. She stormed across the parking lot toward the van.

The doors swung open, and DeeDee leaned out. "Do you have it?" she demanded.

"Have what?" Markus asked.

DeeDee didn't say anything. She stared at Markus, who didn't even look up from his phone.

Alice turned to him. "They sent me in to get the cure for WonderLand."

Looking at Alice, he asked, "There's a cure?"

"That's the rumor." Linc pushed past DeeDee. "Hey, where's Kaleb?"

Alice swallowed. "That's why I'm here. I need a way back in."

"There is no way back in," DeeDee grumbled.

Markus put his phone back in his pocket and pointed at the front door. "For you, maybe." Markus started toward the front of the building, where Joe held open a door. He was halfway there when he turned to ask Alice, "Are you coming?"

Into the depths of the WonderLand crazed world to save Kaleb? Of course, she was.

"Yes."

Chapter 30

Kaleb woke to the thump of pulsing pain in his head. He opened his eyes and then closed them again. Bright white light shone above him, burning his sensitive irises. *Where am I? The last thing I remember is the cold floor against my skin, Alice's eyes, and a need to move pulsing through my skin.*

A tear moved down Kaleb's cheek. He tried to wipe it away, but his hands wouldn't move. A jangle of metal on metal reminded Kaleb he had been handcuffed. To what? It had to be one of the cold metal slabs in Dr. Turtle's lab; it was the only explanation for the bone-chilling cold that spread through his back.

He tried to open his eyes again; this time he did it slower, examining the room through the slits. The room was made of glass. *It has to be one of the cells where Dr. Turtle keeps the volunteers for the drug trials.*

Kaleb's eyes adjusted, and he opened them a little wider. Red lipstick hearts marked the glass walls. He remembered the girl who had drawn the hearts a few hours before when he led Turtle and Gryff out.

Familiar footsteps came toward him, and Kaleb debated whether he should fake sleep or greet his father with open eyes. There was a crash somewhere behind him moments before the footsteps crunched on what sounded like broken glass. Joseph touched Kaleb's forehead.

"I would stand to greet you." Kaleb pulled on his restraints. "But I'm a bit tied up at the moment."

His father didn't say anything.

Someone shuffled around the room, muttering under his breath while opening and closing drawers. It wasn't Joseph. Kaleb thought maybe it was one of the interns.

Cold, clammy hands grabbed his arm, and the tip of a needle pricked his skin. He knew from his time at Red Queen they could be injecting him with anything to exploit his emotions. He tried to jerk his arm away, but the restraints held him in place.

A cool liquid spread through his veins, causing a chill to run through his body. He took stock of his emotions, wondering if he would notice a change.

It didn't take long before his eyes grew heavy. Kaleb struggled to keep them open, but he was falling into the darkness of sleep. Seconds before the drugs took him under, he thought he heard his father's whispered voice settle in his ear. "She's safe."

Kaleb hoped that meant Alice, but he couldn't be sure—not with his father.

Kaleb's last thoughts were of Alice, the sad girl who made him see the good in the world. A smile crossed his lips as he fell into a memory-filled sleep.

"You're in my seat," he grunted.

The girl studied him. He didn't know why he was here. The only thing he could think was it had been too much of a temptation to be so close and not check on her, make sure she was okay. He hoped she would tell him to get lost. Call him a jerk. Do something, besides ignore him. She stood up and exchanged a look with a guy at the table next to her, probably asking him to save her from the creepy stranger bothering her. The guy didn't move. Kaleb shuffled his feet. Guess he didn't get the message.

Alice opened her purse. He looked at the door and back at the girl.

He should go. She would find her phone and call the cops, or worse, pepper spray him. His throat went dry with the memory of the last time his brother had doused him with pepper spray. The blindness and burning lasted longer than it should have.

A story had leaked not too long after the incident at the theater. Leaked wasn't the right word. It was crafted, a way for Red Queen to control the narrative. The thing Ms. Redding didn't count on was a hacker getting a hold of Alice's information and releasing it to the press. Ever since then, Alice had been harassed by reporters.

Not that he looked like a journalist.

Kaleb looked down at his combat boots and black everything, an attempt at hiding his pain. He looked like a wannabe vampire and hated it. It worked for him, though. He didn't deserve to be liked.

To his surprise, Alice pushed a pair of bright pink sunglasses onto her face, and he sighed, only slightly relieved that she didn't pepper spray him. This was it. She's leaving.

It's for the best.

He took a step back, making room for her to walk past him. He was a complete stranger, after all. Even if he knew everything about her, they had never actually met.

Alice turned her back to him, pretending he wasn't there.

Kaleb ran his fingers through his too-long hair and thought about walking away first.

Something told him to keep talking to her. "What are you doing?" he asked.

Alice pushed her short brown hair—which he loved—behind her ears and smiled. Her smile broke through his pain, and his lips twitched, wanting to return the smile, but he held back. He couldn't. Not with this girl.

The bell over the door rang, and a red-haired girl walked in, reminding Kaleb he shouldn't have come here to talk to Alice. He opened his mouth to say as much.

"I don't see it," she said.

"See what?"

"I looked over every inch of this chair, and all I see is 'Alice' written in small black letters," she said.

He tried not to laugh; he was being all broody and moody, and this girl who had every reason to hate the world wanted to make him laugh.

He bit down on his cheek, reminding himself he needed to stay in his bad mood and not get attached, but the smile he wanted to suppress still twitched at the corner of his mouth against his will. "Alice, huh. I don't see it."

Alice rolled her eyes at him and stepped forward to put the pink glasses on him. Her lavender scent surrounded him, chipping at the wall he had built.

"You'll need these." She handed him the pink glasses. "Invisible ink," she whispered.

He laughed at that, a deep-in-the-gut laugh. It was the first time in two years Kaleb had laughed. It was as if a weight had been lifted off his shoulders, like he could be himself with her. Alice had broken through the darkness.

What am I going to do? he asked himself. I shouldn't even be talking to her, but I can't walk away.

Kaleb stared at the chair, trying to find a way to keep her in his life. He knew, deep down, he would have to live with this one moment. He would have to make it last, a single memory he could live on for the rest of his life.

He pointed to a spot in the center of the chair. "Look here, between 'Alice' and 'Alice was here.' Rabbit."

Reid's voice broke into his dream. "Where did you put it?" She slapped him, leaving a stinging tingle on his cheek. "Where's the flash drive?"

Kaleb blinked against the bright light, confused. There was a scuffling noise next to him, and he turned his head toward it. His father had his arms wrapped around a struggling Ms. Redding. A small knife glinted in her right hand.

He tried to pull his arms and legs free, but even without restraints, he wouldn't have gotten far. His limbs felt heavy like lead.

Two men rushed to his father's side, helped push Ms. Redding into a chair, and removed the knife from her hand. Once she was sitting, Joseph bent down and whispered something into her ear. Whatever he said seemed to calm her.

Joseph turned to Kaleb and looked behind him. He spoke to the man who hovered outside of Kaleb's vision. "Do it," he said.

A warm fluid entered Kaleb's body with the familiar prick of a needle, and the world around him turned a slight shade of pink. A giggle built in his chest, and he tried to suppress it.

They'd dosed him with Tillekad, and he knew he would tell them anything.

Kaleb was great at keeping secrets as long as he was wrapped in darkness. Tillekad stripped away that darkness, making him carefree, radiant, joyous, and unable to keep secrets.

Ms. Redding stood up from her chair and hovered over Kaleb, her dark hair shading everything but her eyes. Her eyes reminded him of marbles he had as a kid. "Where is the information you stole?"

Kaleb smiled at her, thinking of his marbles and how he had won them. It was the only time he had beaten Markus at anything. Markus never lost. Of course, Kaleb would never have won if his other brother, Jake, hadn't helped him cheat. Kaleb remembered the look on Markus's face, and the giggle he'd been holding back escaped.

"You gave him too much," the Queen snapped.

The Queen. Kaleb had never thought of her like that before. Why would he do that now? He wrinkled his brow. She had done horrible things, killed people in the name of science.

He tried to fight the drug's effects. The smile was still on his face, but he had stopped giggling.

"Let me try," his father said.

Joseph hovered over him. "Kaleb," he said in a tone he had used to speak to him when he was younger. "Kaleb, please look at me." He met his father's eyes, and he saw a sadness in them that he'd never seen before. "How long have you been working for the Task Force?"

Kaleb tried not to speak, biting his tongue in an attempt to keep his secrets. But the words came tumbling out. "You already know. Since the day in the coffee shop with Alice. Where is Alice?"

"She's safe," Joseph said.

"You know I'm going to marry her one day, but first I have to make things right. Get the cure to people who can help."

Had he told them he had the cure? He clamped his mouth shut. *I don't have the cure. I don't even know if there is one.*

"Did you give the flash drive to the Task Force, Kaleb?" his dad asked.

Kaleb shook his head no. "I never really trusted the Task Force."

"Why?" the Queen asked.

He opened his mouth to answer, and a prick of a needle interrupted his thoughts. The cold liquid that entered his veins reminded him he wasn't in a safe place.

"Turtle, what are you doing?" Ms. Redding demanded.

Dr. Turtle?

Kaleb had gotten him out, watched him leave.

Has he been the one drugging me this entire time? Kaleb tried to turn in the direction he thought the doctor would be, but he was asleep before he could confirm whether it were Turtle. A memory pulled Kaleb from the real world.

It was over, no more hiding a part of himself. Alice was safe from Red Queen Inc., and Reid Redding was on her way to prison. Kaleb planned to tell Alice everything today, on their first real date. He hoped she'd understand and forgive him for his part in her mother's death.

Kaleb had planned a scavenger hunt in Salt City. They would take the train from place to place so Alice could see all his favorite spots. It would also be a great way to see a place Alice had never been to. Then, when it was all over, he would tell her everything. He knew it was selfish to wait until the end, but he wanted one last memory.

In case she didn't forgive him.

He heard someone say his name but didn't want to let go of the dream, not yet.

Alice figured out the third clue. They were at the Fine Art Museum when he got the message. Reid was free, and all charges were dropped. How? He didn't know, but he'd have to find out.

He wasn't free, and Alice wasn't safe. Kaleb put the phone back in his pocket and stared up at the painting, not seeing the picture.

"Everything okay?" Alice asked.

He sighed. "Work. They want me to go in."

Alice stood up, her hand outstretched. "Let's go, then."

"You finish the scavenger hunt." He stood up and pulled her into a hug. "Text me when you get to the end."

"Are you sure?"

"Yes," he said.

He pulled her closer and kissed her forehead knowing this would be the closest he'd ever get to be with her.

Reid was too powerful, and Red Queen Inc. couldn't be brought down. Not without help.

Someone was shaking him. "Kaleb, wake up." His eyes opened, and Alice stared down at him. He reached up, his hands no longer tied down, and pushed a stray strand of her hair so he could see her face.

"I'm dreaming. You can't be here."

Two warm hands helped him into a sitting position. His father came from behind. "She's real, and you have to go,"

Kaleb looked around. Other than the slab he had been lying on, the room was empty. No Reid, no guards, no Turtle. Just Alice and his father. "What's going on?"

Alice and Joseph exchanged a look. "I'll explain everything once we're safe," she said. He tried to stand, but his legs wouldn't listen, and he fell back onto the table.

"You're going to have to help him," his father told Alice.

She moved close enough that he could smell her sweet perfume, different from the sweet floral scent she had worn that day in the coffee shop. It was then he knew this wasn't a dream.

Kaleb tried to stand again. This time, with Alice's help, he was able to shuffle a few feet to the open door. Glass shards crumbled under his steps, Markus stood in front of them, sucking in air. *Had he been running?* Kaleb tried to push Alice behind him, not trusting his brother, but she wouldn't move.

"You have maybe ten minutes before the doors seal for good." Markus looked at Kaleb. "Can you make it to the front doors?"

"Yes." He would have to.

Markus nodded.

Alice turned to Joseph. "What about you?"

"Don't worry; I have a way out," he said.

Kaleb looked at his dad. Scratch marks marred his face, and his clothing was torn.

The sad look in his eyes told Kaleb there was no other way out, not for him. They stepped into the hallway, and his dad pulled him into a hug. "I'm sorry. I should never have brought you into this."

Kaleb moved away from him, confused and unsure of what to say. "Why did you?"

"Everything I have ever done was to protect you and your brothers."

His father kissed Kaleb's forehead and then turned to Alice.

"Take care of him," he said before disappearing back into the room they had left.

With Alice's help, they stumbled drunkenly out the front doors of Red Queen Inc. without incident. They walked into the rain-soaked world. Kaleb stood there for a moment, breathing in the fresh air and letting the rain drip down his face. He never thought he would see the outside world again.

Kaleb turned to Alice. She'd come back for him.

He pulled her close to him, and she smiled. For the first time, Kaleb had hoped that maybe they had a chance.

He pushed her hair from her face.

A male voice made a clearing-the-throat sound behind them. "Umm... We really should get further away from the building before we celebrate," Linc said.

"Linc?" Kaleb pulled his friend into a hug.

Alice screamed.

Kaleb turned back to the double doors.

Reid stood at the door with a gun aimed at Alice.

Kaleb pulled Alice to the ground, using his body to shield her. At the same time, he reached for the gun that wasn't on his hip.

Markus stood over them with a gun in his hand. A shot rang through the cold morning air.

The tang of gunpowder mingled with rain. Kaleb stared at his brother in disbelief. He'd shot the Queen.

"Alice!" Linc rushed toward them.

Blood ran in a river down the wet pavement from beneath Kaleb. Alice looked at him, the color drained from her face, red blood splattered across her pale skin.

Chapter 31

Alice walked down a white hospital hall, dread deep in her belly and the smell of antiseptic overwhelming her senses. *After everything they had gone through...* She couldn't finish that thought. A tan door frame came into view. It surrounded a large piece of glass embedded with tiny crisscrossed scraps of metal. She stopped outside the plain-colored door.

She wasn't ready to go in, but she needed to see his face.

Kaleb lay under a thin yellow blanket in a hospital bed. The beeping of the heart monitor was the only sound in the room. Kaleb was alive. *He protected me, stopped Reid's bullet from going through my skull.* The bullet hadn't caused major damage, but it would take some time for him to heal.

Alice's shoes squeaked on the clean tile floor as she walked into the room. Markus smiled at her approach; he hadn't left Kaleb's side since they'd gotten here two days ago. She sat down in an empty chair next to Kaleb's bed.

"Why don't you take a break," she said. "I'll sit with him."

Markus looked over at his younger brother and then back at Alice. "I should..."

"Go." Kaleb turned his head toward them, a half smile on his face. "I'm fine; besides, you're making me look bad in front of Alice."

Markus smirked. "Little brother, you're doing it all on your own." He stood up and clasped Kaleb's hand. "Besides, she likes me better."

Alice scoffed. "You wish."

A pink tear moved down Kaleb's cheek.

Markus wiped it away without saying anything to his younger brother. He turned to Alice, sadness dancing behind the smile he had plastered on his face for Kaleb's benefit. He was losing his brother to WonderLand, and there was nothing either of them could do about it.

He leaned over Kaleb's bed and whispered something in his ear. He then turned to Alice and pulled her into a tight hug. She could feel the hot tears he had been trying to hide from Kaleb on her cheek. "Don't blame yourself for this. You're the best thing that happened to him and this family." Markus kissed her on the cheek and walked away but not before calling her "sweetheart" loud enough for Kaleb to hear.

Kaleb looked at Alice through shimmering virus-filled eyes. *It's my fault*, she thought. A forced smile moved across her lips. "Hey." She reached under the blanket and took one of his hands. Her fingers rubbed against the rough fabric of the restraints on his wrist. His arms and legs were strapped down to the bed to keep him from hurting himself or anyone else. His skin was hot to the touch. *At least the bleeding stopped.*

Kaleb smiled at her, and the tears Alice had been trying to hold back spilled out.

He squeezed her hand. "Sweet girl, don't cry."

Alice took a deep breath, trying to force herself to feel a calm that wouldn't come. "I left you." She sniffled. "If I hadn't, maybe..."

"Maybe I wouldn't have gotten infected?"

"Yes. No. I don't know." But she did know. Markus had filled her in on Kaleb's plan to get them out. Joe had called Kaleb moments before Kaleb was going to run, forcing him to go back to Red Queen Inc. to protect Alice. *If it weren't for me, Kaleb wouldn't be here. If I had disappeared like he asked me to the first time, he could have escaped.*

Kaleb turned to her, a playful smile on his lips. "Did I ever tell you about the first time I saw you?"

Alice shook her head.

"It was the day at the theater. There was this girl in a thin white dress, jean jacket, and star-covered tights freezing her ass off and not caring. I think I knew somewhere deep down then that if I could spend even a moment with you, it would be worth a lifetime of trouble."

She opened her mouth, a teasing remark to hide her pain from him on her tongue, but there wasn't anything funny to say, not with him lying in a hospital bed dying. She had to do something, respond somehow. She remembered the outfit. She scoffed at her stubbornness and him calling her trouble.

He turned away from her, his gaze focused on the ceiling. Drops of red moved down his cheeks.

Alice grabbed a tissue from a nearby table to wipe them from his face.

"No wise fish would go anywhere without a porpoise," Kaleb suddenly screamed.

The virus was taking hold of him again. The episodes were coming closer together, and he wasn't fighting it. She couldn't understand why he didn't fight it but suspected it had to do with a life he was cheated of. A life filled with love and safety.

The beeping of the heart monitor came faster and louder. Alice dropped Kaleb's restrained hand and moved away from the bed. He tried to yank at the straps on his wrists, causing the thin blanket to fall to the floor.

Why can't he get control of this?

A woman in green scrubs came into the room followed by two men in white. Alice moved past them into the hall. She wanted to stay and talk Kaleb through this, but she didn't have the strength to watch the people scramble for a fix. *Besides, the nurse would just demand I leave.*

WonderLand had been taking Kaleb's sanity more frequently

now, and the doctors had no way to help beyond sedating him. She watched as the two men held Kaleb down while the woman plunged a syringe into his flesh. *It has never been this bad with me. Is this what Dr. Turtle meant when he said this version of the virus was different? There's no way to control it.*

Kaleb stopped fighting, and his heart rate slowed down to a reasonable pace. The doctor waved the two men who had held Kaleb down from the room as she made a note in his chart.

Alice was tempted to go back into the room to ask her all the questions that had been running through her mind even though she knew this woman wouldn't have the answers.

Alice's phone chirped at the same moment the doctor went toward the hall. She ignored it.

The doctor asked Alice for the third time that day, "Are you sure you don't know what he took?"

Alice shook her head. "Like I told the police earlier, he called me, babbled some kind of nonsense, and hung up. I was worried, and I called his brother. We drove around most of the night until we found him like this."

"With a gunshot in his shoulder and no memory of how he got it?"

"Yes."

It was a lie, but they had talked about it. Markus, Linc, DeeDee, and Alice had all agreed it would be best if what was going on inside Red Queen Inc. stayed inside, for now. It was the only way to protect Kaleb. The Task Force would handle the victims of the outbreak until Alice and Kaleb could disappear.

If he survived.

The doctor stared at Alice for a moment as if trying to decide something. "Look, your friend is really bad off. I'll do what I can to make him comfortable, but if he doesn't improve soon... It would be best if he had family nearby."

Alice nodded, worried things weren't getting better. It must be getting worse if the doctor was sharing that much with her. "I'll get his brother."

She looked back at Kaleb, sleeping in the hospital bed; a new blanket covered his restraints. *It's not fair. I got him out.*

Alice turned away from Kaleb and made her way down the hall to find Markus.

Her anger and frustration built with each footfall. *If I had just left like Kaleb asked, this would never have happened.* Alice knew that wasn't true. Reid would have found a way. Maybe she wouldn't have infected him with the virus, but she would have found some way to use him to control Alice. Reid called for her head.

Alice's vision flickered into black and white.

Reid was alive. Markus's shot had missed her by inches, leaving the wannabe queen to rule her kingdom. *It wouldn't take much for me to get back in. Once I was in, I could find a knife. Better yet, I could take Kaleb's knife. A clean cut across the throat would do it. Wet sticky blood would ooze out and cover her throne.*

Wait. No. This isn't right.

She was letting the virus take over. *So what? Let it. Why keep fighting? There's nothing left for me here.*

That's not true; there's Kaleb. I need to stay sane for him.

Alice stopped in the middle of the hall. *Do I need to stay sane for him, though?* She had seen the signs before; Kaleb was getting worse. It wouldn't be long before he was nothing but a ball of rage.

Even if the doctors can keep him alive, his mind would be gone.

Someone limped down the hall toward Alice. She stared at the man with the little white hearts across his red scrubs, not able to believe her eyes. "Dr. Turtle?"

He should still be in Red Queen Inc. The building was supposed to be sealed while the Task Force found a way to deal with the Infected. Dr. Turtle had volunteered to help get Kaleb out and stay behind to help the Task Force address the outbreak.

"Alice, dear, I'm so glad I found you." He clasped her wrist.

"Look, I don't have much time." He turned her hand over. "Where's the bracelet?"

"What?"

"The bracelet I gave you. Tell me you have it."

She looked down at her wrist. "I-I must have taken it off. What are you doing here?"

"Where did you take it off?" he asked urgently.

She shrugged. "The car, maybe."

He patted her hand. "Good, good."

Alice still couldn't believe the odd little man was here. "Dr. Turtle—"

"I know you don't trust me." Dr. Turtle opened his hand, revealing six small disks, three red and three blue.

Alice had no idea what she was looking at. *Alka-Seltzer tablets? Had Dr. Turtle been infected?* She tried to look at his eyes for the telltale shimmer, but he wouldn't meet her gaze. "What is it?"

Dr. Turtle looked at her, astonishment on his face. "I-I-It stops the effects of W-W-WonderLand."

"The what?"

Dr. Turtle started to pace. "I could have done it, should have, but now it might be too late. Four years is a long time, and I did nothing. Well, I did, but no—"

"Dr. Turtle, are you telling me these tablets are the cure to WonderLand?"

His clear virus-free eyes met Alice's. "They'll halt the effects."

Alice expected her vision to flicker to black and white with his words, but it didn't. *Does that mean I can use his scrubs to somehow hurt him? There is red in them, and therefore a weapon. No, that's ridiculous. It's a piece of fabric.* Alice took a step toward him. "How?"

He looked up and down the hall. The only other person in the corridor was an older guy in a hospital gown dragging an IV pole behind him. An IV pole that pulsed red. "Place the tablets on your tongue and let them melt."

She looked back at the IV stand. *Could I get to it before he ran? If*

I did, then what? Use it as a club. No, there is no way to get to the IV pole without alerting the doctor. Alice moved closer to Dr. Turtle, trapping him between her and the wall.

"How long have you had this?" she asked.

Dr. Turtle pulled at the neckline of his shirt, revealing pulsing red finger marks that weren't there yet but matched the shape and size of Alice's hands. *Perfect.* Not too quick, enough to satisfy her need for pain. *If I do it right, no one will know what I've done until it's too late.*

Alice took a step closer, her hands itching to take their place on Dr. Turtle's throat.

"Four years," he stuttered. "I've had the pills for four years."

Strangulation isn't going to work. She needed to see blood. "You... Four years."

Alice reached into her jeans pocket for the knife she had taken from Kaleb. She stroked it and pulled the blade from its confines. Alice smiled as she pressed the knife into the soft flesh of Dr. Turtle's neck. Fresh blood dripped from his throat. "Would you tell me, please, which way I ought to go from here?"

"Alice?" Dr. Turtle swallowed. "You...d-don't..."

Strong arms pulled Alice away from Dr. Turtle, causing the knife to clatter onto the linoleum floor. Alice turned to the imposing form that had ruined a perfectly good kill. Markus let go of her before rushing toward Dr. Turtle and pinning the man against the pale wall. His hands wrapped around the soft flesh of Dr. Turtle's throat.

"What are you doing here?" Markus demanded.

Alice watched as Dr. Turtle struggled to explain between gasps and tried to pry away Markus's fingers. Her mind told her this was wrong while the virus pulled at her to complete her task even if it meant killing Markus to do it.

"One, two, three, four." Alice counted, and with each number, the black-and-white world faded away, bringing color with it. "Markus, stop."

Markus ignored Alice, putting more pressure on Dr. Turtle's throat. Alice stood up and placed her hand on his shoulder.

Markus shrugged it off.

He's going to kill him. Alice tried to think of something to stop Markus. *What had Turtle been talking about?* The virus had a hold of her.

"There's a cure. Markus, did you hear me?" She pulled on his arm. "Dr. Turtle has a cure. We can save Kaleb."

Alice watched Markus's inner struggle between letting the man who had created WonderLand go and saving his brother. Markus let go of Dr. Turtle, who crumbled to the floor, gasping for air.

"Where?"

Alice nodded toward the right pocket of the doctor's scrubs, remembering she had seen him slip the pills back into the pocket at some point during her episode. *I could have killed him.*

Markus grabbed Turtle by the front of his shirt. "How much?"

"Two of each for Alice and one of each for Kaleb."

Alice met Markus's eyes. She hadn't told him that she was infected.

"Why more for Alice?"

Dr. Turtle scoffed. "She's been exposed longer."

Before Markus could ask any more questions, Alice asked, "Will it work?"

"They may work, or they may kill him faster."

Markus lifted him higher, causing Dr. Turtle's legs to dangle a few inches off the floor.

Alice looked around the hall. They had a small crowd gathered around them; it wouldn't be long before security showed up. She nodded.

"Markus, let him down."

"Are you sure?" Markus looked back at her.

"He's not worth it."

Markus dropped Dr. Turtle, took the pills from his pocket, and started down the hall toward his brother's room with the possible cure clutched in his fist. Alice turned to follow him.

Dr. Turtle called out to her. "If it works, there is a side effect. The time you were under the influence of WonderLand will disappear. The memories will be wiped away, and there will be no way to get them back."

If it means saving Kaleb, it's worth it.

CHAPTER 32

Alice sat in the chair next to Kaleb's bed. His heartbeat was getting weaker, and there was nothing that could be done to save him except the tablets Markus had taken from Turtle. The tablets could save him, do nothing, or kill him faster.

"Are you sure?" Markus asked her.

Alice stared down at the tablets, wishing she didn't have to do this. "It's the only way to know for sure."

"What if it works? You won't remember anything from the last four years. You'll be seventeen again."

Would it be so bad? The theater and her mother's death would be gone. Alice looked over at Kaleb; his toes stuck out from under the blanket. If the cure worked, it also meant she would lose Kaleb and everything they built.

"It's the only way to know they work for sure. If nothing happens, then we look for something else."

Markus sighed. "If it does? What am I supposed to tell Kaleb?"

Alice looked over at the hospital bed where he slept, his chest rising and falling with the beeping of the heart monitor. There wasn't any other choice. It was the only way to protect him. She had to disappear. If she wasn't Alice anymore, he couldn't risk his life to protect her.

"If I survive, tell him not to look for me. To live a normal life. He deserves that."

Markus clasped her hand. "It won't stop him from looking, and you know it. He won't stop looking until he finds you."

"He won't find me." A sad smile crossed her lips. "Marci's too good." *Not Kaleb or even Reid Redding herself will be able to find me.*

She moved to stand next to the bed and pulled his car keys from her pocket. As she did, Turtle's bracelet fell to the floor at her feet. Alice picked up the unusual piece of jewelry she had thought was in the car with her blood-soaked clothes and slipped it onto her wrist. She wasn't sure what was so important about it, but if Turtle wanted it, she was going to hold on to it.

Alice laid the keys next to the note she had agonized over for the last hour. The letter would explain her disappearance and encourage Kaleb not to look for her, to move on with his life. She pushed Kaleb's blond curls from his forehead, leaned in, and kissed him. A tear trickled down her cheek. "I thought I might have loved you, but... I'm sorry."

Markus met Alice at the door and handed her two blue and two red pills and instructions on where to meet Marci. "If you do this and it works, there's no going back."

She looked back at the room Kaleb slept in and hoped one day he would forgive her. Then she tossed the pills into her mouth and waited for them to dissolve on her tongue, leaving a minty aftertaste.

It wouldn't matter much longer if he did forgive her. If everything went how she hoped, in ten minutes, she'd have no memory of anything from the past four years. Not even him.

Acknowledgments

To my wonderful and talented writing group, Stacy Codner, Emily Inouye Huey, Sarah Alva, Julie Whipple, and Apryl K.B. Lopez, without you, this dream would never have been possible. Your feedback, support, and skills made me a better writer. Your friendship and support gave me the confidence to share my stories with the world.

To my family: my mom, who is my biggest cheerleader; my dad who never let me give up; and my brother who reminds me daily that he doesn't read but proudly tells everyone he knows his big sister is an author. Thank you for all the love and support. I love you.

To my beta readers, Amanda Markus, Carly Jones, and Terri Daley thank you for taking the time to read and comment. It made this book better. You're amazing. Special thanks to Jade Fisher for the countless hours of early morning meets ups.

I would like to thank everyone at Immortal Works publishing who helped make this possible. I'm lucky to be part of such a marvelous and supportive group of people.

About the Author

Miranda Renae' spent much of her life avoiding reading. Letters were nothing more than a jumbled mess. One day her dad gave her the novel he had just finished. It was full of the kind of suspense and horror she'd only seen in movies—only so much better. From that day on she devoured the written word. No genre was safe.

When Miranda isn't reading or writing, you can find her taking care of a pack of foster kittens or cuddling her two cats Hettie and Courage (who is not brave). For more information, visit Miranda online at mirandarenae.com and follow her on Instagram @_miranda_renae or Twitter/Facebook @mirandrenae42.

This has been an
Immortal Production

www.ingramcontent.com/pod-product-compliance
Lightning Source LLC
Chambersburg PA
CBHW030736110726
47900CB00008B/2331